ALEXEY REMIZOV

On a Field Azure

CLASSICS OF RUSSIAN LITERATURE

ALEXEY REMIZOV

On a Field Azure

HYPERION PRESS, INC.
Westport, Connecticut

Published in 1946 by Lindsay Drummond Limited, London
Hyperion reprint edition 1977
Library of Congress Catalog Number 76-23896
ISBN 0-88355-513-1 (paper ed.)
Printed in the United States of America

Library of Congress Cataloging in Publication Data

Remizov, Aleksei Mikhailovich, 1877-1957.
  On a field azure.

  *(Classics of Russian literature) (The Hyperion
library of world literature)*
  Translation of V pole blakitnom.
  *Reprint of the 1946 ed. published by L. Drummond,
London, which was issued as no. 6 of Russian literature
library.*
  I. Title. II. Series: Russian literature library ; 6.
PZ3.R2849On15 [PG3470.R4] 891.7'3'44 76-23896
ISBN 0-88355-513-1

A NOTE ON THE AUTHOR

By GEORGE REAVEY

ALEXEY REMIZOV was born in 1877, in Moscow. He left Russia in 1921; he was living in Paris when the war broke out and is still there. Alexey Remizov is hardly known to the English reader. He is perhaps as little known to the average Soviet reader; for although a Russian writer, he is not strictly speaking a Soviet writer and his works have not been republished in the Soviet Union since the early 'twenties when he turned his back on the Revolution and went into emigration. And unlike some writers of the early emigration, such as Alexey Tolstoy for example, he never succeeded or perhaps even tried to build himself a bridge of return to his native land, but continued his literary activities abroad—mainly in Paris. This is all the stranger because he was fundamentally a very Russian writer, without any traits of the cosmopolitan, and hardly at ease in foreign surroundings.

His departure in 1921 from the revolutionary scene, on the eve of the foundation of a new school of Russian writers, came as a shock to his admirers, disciples and a number of younger writers who had been influenced by his works. In an account of those days published in the Soviet Union in 1944, the Soviet writer Konstantin Fedin says: "But here suddenly the rumour spread that Remizov had fled abroad. At first none of the younger people believed it. They thought everything would be explained, that he would reappear as suddenly as he vanished, that he had gone somewhere into the wilds, to isolate himself and rest. Zoshchenko used to say to me that the flight of such a man into foreign lands was unnatural, like the migration of a fish into the mountains." This shock led to a reassessment of Remizov's work, and as Fedin says: "Then, in that year of Remizov's emigration from Petersburg, all his complexity as a writer in our eyes was extraordinarily simplified, becoming essentially a bare formal manifestation of style." This is still the position today as far as the Soviet Union is concerned. Remizov is neither published nor normally discussed, although a number of other older writers have been revived in the past ten years.

While Remizov's influence waned after 1921, it was nevertheless considerable in the preceding decade, when it affected writers as varied as Alexey Tolstoy and Zamyatin, and made itself felt in the early revolutionary novels of Pilnyak, Vesioly, and Malyshkin. When referring to his second book of verse, *Beyond Blue Rivers* (1918) in his *Brief Autobiography* (1944), Alexey Tolstoy says: "*Beyond Blue Rivers* was the result of my first acquaintance with Russian folklore and Russian folk traditions. In this I was helped by A. Remizov, M. Voloshin and Vyatcheslav Ivanov . . . "

Russian folklore was indeed the heart and core of Remizov's world as a writer and a man. He was steeped in this atmosphere and in these traditions. He was not content to use the folk element in his work, but created around himself a visible world of fantasy, and this coloured and often distorted the real world he lived in and wrote about. Fittingly enough, he was in appearance and manner, gnome-like,—small, large-headed, bright-eyed, slightly humped, broad-featured, big-mouthed. Thus I saw him in Paris. Fedin gives us another glimpse of him in Petersburg: "A man, stooping and having something in common with the Hunchbacked horse, is running along the Nevsky slightly bending at the knees, glancing piercingly from under his glasses, in a little coat and hat,—it was Kukovnikov, no other,—the man with this whimsical name in which Alexey Michailovich Remizov dressed himself up many years later in Paris, among the number of other pseudonyms and guises which he adopted and in which he masqueraded."

Among other important influences behind Remizov's work are Dostoyevsky and Lieskov. From the former he derived an almost excessive sensitivity to suffering and a visionary turn of mind; from the latter, the racy idiomatic speech of the peasantry and the provinces, and this Remizov developed and pushed almost to an extreme. There was also Gogol and his sense of the grotesque. Another more contemporary influence was that of the Symbolists who dominated the Russian literary scene at the turn of the century and well after (Gorky was of course a rising star who was going another way). There were two main trends of the Symbolist movement: one more purely "aesthetic" and "ivory-tower"; the other mystico-philosophical with a sense of impending catastrophic events. But one feature common to both sections was the stress on the musicality of the phrase which echoed Verlaine's "rien que de la musique." This tendency as it developed, especially in the prose of Andrey Biely, led to the introduction of the "musical phrase" into prose. This had the effect of disintegrating the traditional narrative style of the classical and realist story and novel, and of substituting in their place, a lyrical or semi-lyrical text compounded of symbols, verbal images and associations, musical phrases and song-like refrains. Many of the early revolutionary novels such as Pilnyak's *Naked Year*, Malyshkin's *Fall of Dair*, Artiom Vesioly's *Russia of Fire*, about the civil war and the first days of the Revolution, strongly reflect this trend and are pitched in a lyrical key. Remizov was in many ways the pioneer of this style in prose, but he managed to combine it often enough with glimpses of penetrating realism, leaving it to Andrey Biely to soar into higher and more abstract spheres of verbal music. If Biely did not get as far as Joyce did in his *Finnigan's Wake*, it was probably mainly because he kept to Russian words only and never attempted an international vocabulary, and also because he was too much tied to his recurrent philosophical symbols.

By 1917, Remizov was already a writer of established reputation and the master of a unique style that was much quoted by writers of that decade. By this time he had also to his credit a large body of work (his first book, *The Pond*, was published in 1907); among it are *Princess Mymra* (1908), *The Clock* (1908), *Stratilatov* (1909), *Sisters of the Cross* (1910), *The Fifth Pestilence* (1912), *Petushok* (1911). In 1910, he had also begun his novel

On a Field Azure, the story of the upbringing and development of a young girl, Olya,—a charming portrait with deft touches of characterisation but told by no means in the conventional style of the realistic novel. *On a Field Azure* was to prove but the first part of a trilogy (the other two being *Destiny* and the *Face of Fire*, and all three were finally published in one volume as *Olya* (1927)); and he was to finish it later. It was not published until 1922 when he was already in emigration. By contrast with his earlier works, the style of *On a Field Azure* is more restrained and mature.

In most of these works, and especially in the earlier ones, one cannot help being struck by Remizov's sensitivity and almost morbid Dostoyevskian sense of pity for the victims of life's miseries. But had Remizov not himself written: "Dostoyevsky is Russia. And without Dostoyevsky there is no Russia." That is of course a point of view with which Gorky, for one, violently disagreed, and Gorky's opinion is still the criterion of the Russia of today.

Another feature of Remizov's writing is his passion for the *word*, the colloquial Russian-Slavonic word as distinct from the German and French "intruders." This he derived in the first place from Gogol and Lieskov (the latter especially a master of the racy colloquial Russian which was spoken in the provinces and was far removed from the polite drawing-room conversations of Petersburg); but he pursued his passion further, and eager research among old texts and documents, in the Slavonic liturgy and folklore, yielded a wealth of new-found words and turns of speech, as well as, of course, a wealth of erudite lore which Remizov loved interpolating or making use of in his fiction. The best illustration of this passion is perhaps his publication *Russia in Writ*, a collection of traditional documents with commentaries by himself and the fact that he revived for his own use the cursive hand-writing style of the 17th century. In his revival of the colloquial style, Remizov was in a sense preparing the ground in this domain for more left-wing writers like Mayakovsky and Khlebnikov, but he was not really in line with them spiritually; his researches had to some extent rooted him too deeply in the past of his country; and his love of the old word and what lay behind it made him sometimes indulge in pure archaisms. This, and his craft in arranging the texture of his prose, interpolations and all, gave his prose that stylised and ornate appearance which, indeed, with its colloquial and traditional savour, is its main characteristic. Gorky did not like this style. In a letter to Konstantin Fedin, reprinted in the latter's *Gorky With Us*, he writes: "Remizov is a man absolutely poisoned with Russian words, he interprets each word as an image and because of that his word-writing is formless,—it is not live-writing, but precisely word-writing. He writes not stories, but psalms."

But there is a greater variety and range in Remizov than may appear at first sight. He had delved into provincial life (*The Clock, Stratilatov, The Fifth Pestilence*), into the city life of Moscow based on his childhood impressions (*The Pond*), into a corner of Petersburg life (*Sisters of the Cross*), combining a note of strident realism with a symbolical and mystical approach. And behind it all was the texture of his folklore which he wove not only into his larger works but to which he also gave separate expression in many characteristic tales and stories published under some of the following titles: *Tales of the King of the Apes, Asyka, Tales of the Russian People, St. Nicholas' Parables, Trava Murava*, and others. Among his other works are the *Chronicle of 1917, Lament for the Ruin of Russia, The Noises of the Town*, and *Rozanov's Letters* (he was a close friend of Rozanov, that strangest of Russian writers).

As Fedin says: "The tenderness felt by Remizov for the Russian soil, ... combined in itself passion and femininity, and was his real essence as a writer. No grimace, no idiocy or clowning could hide this principal, serious aspect of his art. It seemed as if he had sunk into the Russian soil so deeply that no force could dig him out. . . . ."

My last vision of him was in Paris before the war: that of a not very happy gnome-like exile from his native forests (it is significant that he turned to Brittany and her druids for some of his later inspirations). He was engaged at the time in compiling a collection of dreams such as had occurred in Russian fiction, especially in Gogol, Turgenev and Dostoyevsky. He had already published *Dreams*, a collection of everyday dreams retold by himself. He was much preoccupied with the dream and he made use of it in his own work. The dreams he was working on at this time, he was illustrating himself. His love of the manuscript is shown in the fact that he had copied out these dreams in his fine cursive hand and, when his illustrations were added, the whole made a manuscript worthy of an earlier age. It was amusing to see that the Russian "chort" or devil—who is a sly and very earthy physical character and is not at all a satanic personage—kept intruding into these illustrations (he appears, of course, in Gogol's *Christmas Eve* and many a folk tale, and Remizov had very much adopted him). He was often enough a "priapic chort"; and every now and again he peeps out from a page of Remizov and one is given a feeling of something weird and strange, and very different from his habitual sense of playfulness and humour. Thus Remizov is a writer of whims and moods, by turns sentimental, fantastic, erudite, humorous, tormented or morbidly realistic; but he is above all elusive. He is not always everyone's cup of tea. But he can also be a writer of great charm and sensibility as in *On a Field Azure*; and he has certainly enriched the literary language of Russia as well as set it at one time the problem of a stylised prose, which has since been dismissed as an undesirable manifestation of "formalism."

PROLOGUE

I

MANY pilgrims wandered in Vatagino and through Vatagino—
two roads lay through the village: one to Kiev, the other to
Chernigov.

The pilgrims put up for the night at the Il'menevs.

Alexander Pavlovich gave orders that everyone should be
admitted: there was a room like that in the house with benches
and broken cupboards where the pilgrims were given food and
drink and where they could shelter for the night.

The half-wit, Karl Karlovich, wandered about the village.
He was frightening and seemed all covered with bristles—Olya
was afraid of him. Karl Karlovich used to say something about
Olya, only you couldn't understand what it was, and he never
referred to her brother, Misha, except as "a ward in the court of
the nobility," and he would laugh, putting out his long tongue.

Shtunya, the vagabond, stumbled about too, only for some
reason she was never allowed in the house.

Before Easter Olya used to smuggle out some Easter cake
for her.

Shtunya had a bad reputation: they said she was *unclean*.

Once when Natalya Ivanovna was nursing Olya's youngest
sister Tanya, she was walking in the garden and she noticed a
little package tied with ribbon on the path; she picked it up,
opened it, and there was blood on the slip of paper. Next day
she fell ill: five abscesses appeared one after the other on her
breast.

A bit of paper with blood on it, flung down as a "bait" is a
powerful spell and people do suffer seriously from it.

It must have been of something like this that they suspected Shtunya.

Not a few unclean things occurred in the village and Vatagino's Father Evdokim was always unravelling tangles with the sign of the cross at the sprouting of the corn and at threshing time, from which a considerable profit came in.

Mikitka-the-Snake, the deaf-mute, was not allowed in the house either, but he always slipped in cunningly to beg under the windows: Mikitka growled menacingly, pointing now at the earth, now at his breast, now at the sky.

It was fearful to see him, he looked so malignant and terrifying.

Once he was driven from the yard and it was raining. But he wouldn't go away and stood wailing at the fence.

Olya was seized with fright. She felt that he would certainly do them an ill turn and immediately, now, whilst he was wailing so, pointing at the earth at his breast and at the sky.

In spite of the rain, Olya went out and gave the dumb man fifteen kopeks and the dumb man moved on.

"Where have you been to?" Natalya Ivanovna asked sternly.

"Just for a walk," Olya answered and though her dress was wet and her feet were wet through, Olya said this in such a way and looked in such a way that Natalya Ivanovna did not even scold her.

Except for Shtunya and the deaf-mute Mikitka, everyone was allowed in.

Alexander Pavlovich refused a beggar only once, and this happened on the day of the Nativity of Our Lady during the festival of the patron saint of Vatagino.

Olya remembers that day.

After dinner Olya and Misha were sitting under the early fruit-trees and an apple fell down. Olya was delighted, she snatched up the apple and began running to the house with her marvel: they take the hastings down in June and in September they're a great rarity. But on the way Misha snatched the apple from Olya's hand and began boasting that it was he who had found this wonder! And however much Olya insisted that it was she who had noticed it first and picked it up, no one believed Olya—everyone believed Misha.

As happens in summer, thunder began to threaten, it grew very dark and everything was hushed as it is hushed only before a heavy thunderstorm, and a beggar came; he asked to be allowed in and was refused.

The storm began.

Olya was not afraid of thunder but falling in with her mother's wishes she always had to be safe on the bed wrapped up from head to foot in silk dresses, but this time she felt lonely and stifled.

Alexander Pavlovich was upset for a very long time, he blamed himself so much that he had not let the beggar in—he had refused a man in rain and storm.

Olya herself was kindhearted, a welcome guest, the Vatagino peasant women called her: not knowing how to help the old woman Mitrikha—she heard about Mitrikha from old nurse Fatevna—Olya used to fetch macaroni from the cupboard and take it to the old woman so that she could make herself macaroni soup.

Each year vagabonds and pilgrims visited the Il'menevs' house more and more. There were good people amongst them, they told good tales and sang melancholy songs so clearly; light and tranquillity entered the house with them. But some were strange, squint-eyed so that it was frightening when they crossed the threshold of the old house.

Once a nun knocked at the gates.

They led her into the house: she asked for a night's lodging.

Natalya Ivanovna glanced at her and something at once welled up in her—she didn't like the nun, didn't want to let her stay the night.

Alexander Pavlovich broke in:

"What, not let her in? You can't: she's going on a pilgrimage." So they let her in.

When they gave the nun a samovar so that she could have

tea to drink all night, Olya ran into the strange room and quickly ran out again.

"Mummy, it's a man!"

Natalya Ivanovna locked herself into the nursery with the children and didn't sleep all night.

"Go to sleep, little one!" But Olya couldn't sleep either.

"No, the nun is walking about in there!"

For the nun was not asleep either. She paced the room the whole night long and left at daybreak.

"That nun must have been plotting something evil," Natalya Ivanovna said afterwards, "look, how she frightened the child!"

Alexander Pavlovich himself decided to go on a pilgrimage.

When he had been nineteen he was very ill, and on getting better he made a promise—now he decided to fulfil it.

Along with nurse Fatevna who had made pilgrimages to the sacred places more than once, and with all the old men and women of Vatagino and Mezheninka, he set out on foot for Kiev.

II

Alexander Pavlovich was thin and tall, his beard was white and long, his dark blue eyes were steadfast and whenever he smiled Olya felt merry.

He spent all the time alone in his room (his study was next to Granny Anna Mikhailovna's, his mother's room) either reading old books in leather bindings or writing or praying. Sometimes late in the evening he would go into the ballroom and sit there alone in the dark. He never went out, at one time he used to go to church and then he stopped going to church too.

Not so long ago a great many visitors used to come to the Il'menevs' at Vatagino and sit over cards till morning—the ombre tables were never opened now.

And only when the children sat playing at "kings" or "mouche," particularly "mouche," if he happened to be passing,

Alexander Pavlovich would always stop and begin helping and
the one he helped would be sure to win.

Olya liked it when he helped her—Olya adored playing
cards—but unless they cheated she always lost, but with the
right cards it would be "King!" safely without cheating.

And how cheerful Alexander Pavlovich had once been!

The Il'menevs' neighbour, old Mrs. Borov, would tell how
he used to come home from his regiment, and what presents he
used to bring everyone: sometimes he'd bring his youngest sister
Nadezhda twelve pairs of short boots in different coloured fine
leather! And in winter when he'd harness the horses to the
enormous sledge, collect all the neighbours and go riding off—
you'd never feel a dull moment with him. And how he joked!
And he sang so well and told such good tales you'd sit listening
till cockcrow.

And Mrs. Borov would also tell how Natalya Ivanovna fell
in love with Alexander Pavlovich.

They were out visiting in Vatagino, Mrs. Borov, Alexander
Pavlovich's sister Nadezhda Pavlovna, and Alexander Pavlovich
who was engaged.

"And when it was time to go back Natalya Ivanovna spent
such a long time saying goodbye to Alexander Pavlovich, that
though there was no snowstorm when they began their farewells
a snowstorm came before they finished—they lost their way and
only just got home."

Maria Petrovna Vol'sky, Natalya Ivanovna's cousin who
frequently stayed with them in Vatagino, used to recall often,
how Alexander Pavlovich would sit playing cards all the evening
at balls, but just as soon as they began playing the mazurka he'd
drop his cards and be off to the ballroom.

"All the young girls fought over Alexander Pavlovich!" Maria
Petrovna would say, gulping hard, "as soon as they struck up
the mazurka their hearts stood still—would Alexander Pavlovich come up?"

And what rare holidays and balls he held during the years
of his command!

Sometimes when the children were playing he would sit down in an armchair and begin to catch them with his arms.

The Il'menevs' old house with its towers was illuminated—moving islands floated on the pools and drifting monograms, the alleys were lit up in the garden, fireworks, rockets, music. "Guests came from three provinces," they would say reminiscently, "they danced or went out on the balcony to admire the beautiful scene, and there on the balcony they had musicians and singers to delight the guests with music and song."

The memory of the Il'menevs' balls lingered on for many years.

"They said that the host himself made preparations a month ahead, and ladies would spend two months getting their gowns sewn, so that you can imagine how grand and fresh and exquisite the dresses were!"

Only the horses were left now of all the things which had offered amusement in those days.

Alexander Pavlovich liked horses: he never struck them with his whip and they obeyed him,—he talked to them in a special kind of way and stood up for them.

Olya was always asking to be taken for a ride—she liked it so, the horses never ran away and when they raced ahead she felt inspired. And Alexander Pavlovich took her with him both across country and to Mezheninka to her favourite Granny, Tatiana Alexeyevna.

Alexander Pavlovich was seldom with the children.

Sometimes when the children were playing he would come out of his room, sit down in an armchair and begin to catch them with his arms—they squealed and ran and struggled, but he would still catch them all without even getting up.

And somehow it felt so gay, better than any other game.

Olya and Misha were always together: they spent whole days in the garden playing travellers, building huts out of wooden boards under the plum tree. They differed in one thing only: Olya used to go to her father's study, Misha never.

And how glad he would be when Olya ran in!

He would stroke her head:

"My small kitten!"

And no one else called her that, no one caressed her like that or spoke such words to her:

"My small kitten!"

Olya would perch on the arm of his chair, and he, catching the nail of one of his fingers on to the nail of his thumb—Alexander Pavlovich had this habit—he would talk to her so well, no one else talked to her like that.

He told Olya about Christ, how Christ came down to earth, and he taught Olya to love Christ and to love men.

"And then Christ will love you and you will be happy!"

And when Olya passed on to him that old Nurse Fatevna had told her that she was not an ordinary girl but a general's daughter, Alexander Pavlovich remarked sternly that Olya must not be proud because of that.

"If you are asked whose daughter you are, you must say simply: the daughter of an honest man."

And he told Olya that it didn't matter who was thought first and who last in the world.

"It's only important who is first before God."

Sometimes Olya would find her father at prayer with her Granny Anna Mikhailovna: and they let her stop with them, and Olya said her prayers too.

There was one thing which Alexander Pavlovich could not bear—money. And whenever the conversation turned on money he would alter completely, get up and walk out.

Once when he received a very large sum—they said this was some sort of money he should have received long long ago for the peasants' land—he came home from town, put this money on the table and fell down.

III

The Il'menevs' house was rich, its white towers gazed beyond the wide expanses of the meadows into the great steppe; the furnishings and decorations of their forbears were splendid, silver dark with age, dull gold, costly velvet and noiseless carpets, faded cupids and flowers on the ceilings, heavy chandeliers, mirrors, ancient portraits in the sitting-room, in the drawing-room, in the portrait gallery—the walls were strong and the earth beneath them strong—the establishment was permanent—and the bronze figured clock on the mantel had ticked away the minutes clearly without losing, for whole centuries.

"The house in which there is no peace shall perish!" Alexander Pavlovich would not infrequently say.

One night when the conversation between the father and the mother grew louder than usual, Olya jumped out on to the balcony and wanted to shout: "Good people, help!" thinking that hearing her voice they would come and do something, and this thing which filled the house with gloom and trouble would go away. But she didn't cry out, didn't call them—she didn't know herself why not: perhaps the wisdom of her heart told her that no one, no kind of people could help in this—and she went quietly back to the nursery.

"The house in which there is no peace shall perish!" Alexander Pavlovich repeated.

In the evening when Alexander Pavlovich passed through the dining-room where the children usually sat, and made the sign of the cross over each, saying, "Christ be with you"—that meant that he would not come out into the rooms any more and would read in his study, pray and go to bed.

"Good night," Olya said, and though she was used to this, knowing that she alone said anything when they took leave of their father, yet this time she felt both sad and lonely.

That night a loud noise woke Olya.

She ran out on to the porch. Old Nurse Fatevna was sitting there. Olya sat down beside her.

Nurse Fatevna said that Alexander Pavlovich had fallen ill all of a sudden and they wanted to send for the doctor, but he wouldn't let them:

"If God helps, then well and good, but doctors can't help me anyway."

"I've noticed for a long time now, Olyushka, that a mole has been digging up the earth!"

And the old woman fell silent.

Olya sat and shivered.

When things settled down again in the house and Fatevna led Olya back to the nursery, Alexander Pavlovich was already a little better.

"You see, Natalya Ivanovna, I knew it was just make-believe!" Olya heard as she lay in bed: this was Aunt Maria Petrovna, who was staying at Vatagino.

And Olya wanted to get up and shout aloud over the whole house, now at once and so that everyone should hear:

"That's not true! He can't be pretending, he never pretends!"

But she didn't shout—she didn't make up her mind; and why not? Or perhaps something told her—the wisdom of her heart—that that would not help.

Alexander Pavlovich was ill for a week and then he hardly even came out into the rooms, instead he sat in his own room—and in the evenings the light did not go on in his study.

"The house in which there is no peace shall perish!" Olya remembered, and suddenly she began to tremble, as she had trembled that night when she sat in nothing but her nightdress with Fatevna in the porch.

IV

Granny Tatiana Alexeyevna, Natalya Ivanovna's mother, came to Vatagino. And though she often came to Vatagino and the children went on long visits to her in Mezheninka, her arrival was always an event.

Tatiana Alexeyevna was their favourite Granny.

Natalya Ivanovna was always saying to the children:

"Love your Granny, children!"

And she would tell Olya particularly:

"Granny loves you best."

And it was true, Olya was her favourite: Granny let her do anything she liked and only gazed lovingly on whatever tricks she played, whatever wonders she worked, her favourite red-cheeked, grey-eyed granddaughter, and she stood up for her if Natalya Ivanovna was vexed with her over anything.

And in her turn, when Granny was going home to Mezheninka, Olya would start to howl so you could hear her all over the house.

And Granny to stop Olya crying would give her a twenty-kopek coin to play with, and lots of coins—without end! She would keep pressing them into Olya's tiny hand until she drove away, more often than not after some deception.

When their favourite Granny arrived everything seemed to change—the day was more lovely and the night seemed more starry.

From morning to night the children never left Granny's side and Olya especially.

Alexander Pavlovich came into the dining-room for tea and said he had just seen the devil in the drawing-room.

"The devil."

Tatiana Alexeyevna pursed her lips—she always did that when she was angry.

"You are always seeing devils. Why have I never seen the devil!"

"He's always leading you by the nose, so he doesn't have to show himself to you," Alexander Pavlovich answered.

"My horses!" Granny suddenly shouted angrily.

And however much Natalya begged, however much Olya howled, she wouldn't listen, but got her things together and went away there and then, threatening never to set foot in Vatagino again.

Troubled as things were before, now it grew frightening in the Il'menevs' old house.

Everything was hushed, as if everyone had lost his voice and only the figured bronze clock on the mantel ticked away the minutes clearly as before, without losing, as it had done for centuries.

Olya, huddled in a corner, would cry whole evenings at a time.

Her tears were bitter and oppressive: she was sorry for her favourite Granny and for her mother and father. And as she pitied them her heart seemed to tell her that it wasn't anyone's fault: not Granny's fault, or Mummy's or Daddy's.

"Granny, she's like that, our favourite Granny, Mummy loves us children more than anything else and doesn't want anything else, Daddy loves us but he loves something else too."

But what it was she couldn't imagine.

The tears were bitter and oppressive—nothing would help and there was no way of helping.

"The house will perish where there is no peace!" old Nurse Fatevna repeated, grunting as she wandered in the shadows.

And her words, her grunts and her whispering—their old grey nurse, who had nursed all the children and Alexander Pavlovich himself—became unbearable. The tears dried on one's eyes, as if they were being burnt, and that made it more hurting still.

Alexander Pavlovich went to Mezheninka and brought Granny back—Granny forgave him.

With his door shut, he spent days and nights alone in his room.

Only Olya ran in to see him as before.

And how glad he was when Olya came running.

"My small kitten!" he said to her quietly and gently, and he caressed her as no one else caressed her and called her:

"My small kitten!"

V

And so it happened that amidst various other words and discussions Olya once heard a strange word and one she couldn't understand spoken about her father:

"Insane."

Olya thought a lot over this strange word she couldn't understand, and from the confusion of things gone by, days which she had never forgotten rose up before her.

It was three years ago—Olya had been quite small then: a three-year-old—in the autumn. Natalya Ivanovna was not in Vatagino: she was taking Irena to Kiev to the High School. Their favourite Granny remained at home with the children. Andryushka, Mitrikha's grandson, gave Olya and Misha rides in the wheelbarrow all day long about the yard—they had a fine time. At night Granny went to bed in the nursery with the children, and before she lay down, for some reason she fastened the door with the hook and barricaded it with a table and chairs. And in the middle of the night they suddenly woke the children, dressed them, and quickly led them out of the house into the servants' quarters at the bottom of the garden. In the morning Granny strictly forbade them to go into the house. But Olya disobeyed, and ran in.

Alexander Pavlovich, with his hands behind his back, was walking up and down the ballroom and saying something in a loud voice, and by the mantelpiece, under the clock, sat a strange dark gentleman.

Alexander Pavlovich was delighted to see Olya.

"God is in this!" he said, giving Olya a little crystal perfume flask full of water.

Olya took the flask: it pleased her very much—it was such a little one, with so many facets and a long neck.

"Do you know how to cross yourself? Not only like this, but like this too!"

And making the sign of the cross on his breast and on his back, Alexander Pavlovich suddenly looked intently at Olya and in amazement exclaimed:

"You are Ivan the Warrior!"

At this point Nionila the maid led Olya away.

Olya afterwards heard people saying that Alexander Pavlovich had pushed his mother, Granny Anna Mikhailovna from the porch, and the nanny with Lena as well (Lena was still a baby in arms) and he drove out old Nurse Fatevna with the broom.

Natalya Ivanovna returned at dinner time and moved the children to their neighbours the Lupechevs: she went with the children.

They said at the Lupechevs that Alexander Pavlovich was running about the yard and standing on the well.

In the evening Father Evdokim came to the Lupechevs.

Natalya Ivanovna was crying.

"Father," she begged him, "look and see how they bind Alexander Pavlovich: don't let them tie him too hard!"

Father Evdokim made the sign of the cross over her and told her again and again not to worry.

Next day when they returned home and went in, everything in the rooms was upside down: all the furniture was broken, the window panes smashed in and large bottles which had held wood oil lay scattered about the floor along with gold buttons from a uniform.

Natalya Ivanovna wept the whole evening.

And Olya amused herself with some little red plates which Natalya Ivanovna had brought her for a present from Kiev, and with that perfume flask—such a little one with so many facets and a long neck.

Their favourite Granny stopped in Vatagino with them.

Towards the end of autumn Natalya Ivanovna took Misha and Olya to the provincial capital Pokidosh, seventy-five miles from Vatagino.

"Daddy wants to see you."

In the doctor's flat in the town Alexander Pavlovich came to meet them: he was very pleased and kissed them and wept.

They lived through the winter alone.

Just before Easter preparations began afresh.

"We'll go to fetch Daddy and bring Daddy home," Natalya Ivanovna told Misha and Olya.

And when they were returning home—Olya remembered—the first spring rain was falling and they were all so happy!

And Olya remembered how her father showed the wounds on his wrists and feet from the rope with which he was bound, and said he was glad of that:

"Because Christ was wounded."

On Easter Day Alexander Pavlovich went into the village to the peasants who had bound him, he wanted to exchange the Easter greeting with them, but the men hid: they were afraid.

At first Olya was afraid too: old Nurse Fatevna told how Alexander Pavlovich broke a bench when they were binding him.

* * * * *

And so one by one those troubled, unforgettable days passed before Olya, and remembering them and pondering over that strange word she couldn't understand, "insane," Olya somehow felt in her heart of hearts that it was very terrible and—very good that her father was not the same as everyone else.

"There isn't anyone else like him!"

CHAPTER ONE

I

EVERY day a little rabbit brought Granny Anna Mikhailovna sweets and Granny gave them to Olya.

Only he was such a strict rabbit: not once did he bring any sweets before dinner! And however many times Olya ran into her Granny's room to enquire whether the rabbit had been or not, the answer was always the same:

"Not yet."

But as soon as Olya finished dinner she would run to Granny and Granny would put the sweets in her hand straight away: so the rabbit had been.

Olya had never seen this rabbit herself and had only heard about him from Granny but she had no doubts about the rabbit coming and bringing sweets—of course he did: every day there were some sweets waiting and not only after dinner but in the evening too.

Granny Anna Mikhailovna was old, she never left her room, just sat up in her bed—she had bad legs. Olya knew this and was always careful: she never touched Granny's legs.

It was hot in Granny's room, as hot as in a Turkish bath.

Granny was in a white cap, and she was little, but above the bed there hung a portrait—Granny when she was young—there she was rosy and big and she wore a beautiful shawl, all in flowers. It was hard to believe that it was Granny in the portrait and Granny on the bed.

But Olya believed it—Granny had explained to her—there in the portrait she was "Mummy" and she had been big and rosy, and now she was "Granny" and had become little and old.

Granny prayed all day and in the evenings she told Olya fairy tales about the grey wolf and about the fox and about the frogagog who sings songs. And Granny also told about when Olya was little and what she did then: about how Olya started walking on her two feet when she was nine months old, and how she asked to go very early; how they used to undress Olya and let her run naked about the room—her little body looked as if it was bound together, it was all over little bandages; how Olya kissed very well and spat very well—her Uncle Alexey Ivanovich gave her a gold piece for every kiss and every spit.

And Granny told Olya about her father Alexander Pavlovich, how he was small, how he studied, how he joined the regiment of Prince Karl of Prussia and went to the wars, and how there was an earthquake then and the holy lamp before the ikons quivered.

And about Olya's great-grandfather, Peter Mikhailovich—he was powerful and daring.

"He tore a wild wolf in two, that's what he was like!"

And about grandfather—her husband Paul Petrovich—how strict he was.

"Whenever he happened to have to go to town on business, each time he demanded that on his return a plate of soup would be ready for him on the table—and beware if there was no soup or if the soup was not hot!"

And how for safety's sake they had mounted men ready at fifteen miles distance from each other from the house to the town, and how afterwards Paul Petrovich suddenly developed a mental disorder.

"And it was sad," Granny recalled, "his unfortunate illness was incomprehensible. He was always melancholy and pre-occupied, didn't like to talk to anyone or go anywhere, received no one and he would always tell everyone that for him nothing was pleasant and amusing and that for him life was intolerable. Every trifle upset and disquieted him, he slept very little, but felt no pain or weakness and he would always tell everyone he was well. And the doctors refused to treat him, they said time would cure him: his illness and mental grief were spiritual and they could not cure that."

And Granny told her how terribly Grandfather Paul Petro-vich died—he cut his throat! And at that time she slept for six weeks from the horror of it and only woke because her daughter Lizochka touched her with her small hands. Lizochka died too and only "Daddy" was left and then Olya came:

"A swan brought Olya, he knocked with his wing on the window and put her under the clock by the fireplace."

This was in the month of July at sunrise on the fourth day of the month, the day of St. Andrew of Crete and the Manifesta-tion of the Most Blessed Virgin in Perga.

Granny was married when she was fourteen and she had fourteen children, and her dowry consisted of fourteen trunks bound with wrought-metal clasps full of goods.

"You couldn't count all the names of all the things," Granny liked to say, "you won't have enough fingers: well, try——"

two ikons, one of the Saviour and one of the Mother of God,
three trunks of money,
a silver-gilt ducat,
silver soupspoons and teaspoons, three dozen of each,

a dozen silver trays,
with seven goblets on each tray, six gilt and one not,
a gold ring,
three large dishes,
three bowls with lids,
a fox fur coat trimmed with capucine,
an underskirt with a decorated border,
a satin blouse,
a dressing-gown trimmed colour of capucine,
an underskirt and blouse of tabby taffeta,
a cherry-coloured cotton underskirt,
a fur coat of hareskin covered in red kafa,
a cloth Polish surcoat, cherry red,
another cloth one in blue,
a lambskin coat covered in cherry cloth,
a little lambs-coat covered in blue cloth,
a camelot dressing-gown in green,
another of red camelot,
a blouse and underskirt of green repp,
an underskirt of Venetian calamanko,
two in a wool mixture,
two linen ones,
a thin baize apron,
and a white taffeta one,
a grey flannel blouse,
a cherry flannel blouse with little spots,
a blouse of red kafa,
a white silk striped shawl for everyday,
another with a fancy border,
a third of thick red material,
a fourth of deep rose taffeta,
a fifth of green taffeta,
two cotton ones a little worn,
two taffeta corsets,
three trunks of table cloths spun in patterns and designs,
embroidered hand towels,

spun lengths of cloth for kerchieves,
white handkerchieves,
aprons,
thirty-two lady's shifts,
eight man's shirts,
three trunks of flaxen linen and rough hemp,
an ornamental hanging,
large pillow-cases,
small pillow-cases,
linen sheets,
one embroidered sheet,
white shawls,
plaids,
a carpet,
and in the fourteenth and last trunk:
a calico coverlet,
twenty-two sashes backed with silk,
and six sashes more,
ten lace aprons,
an eiderdown,
two big pillows,
two smaller ones,
two smaller ones still,
ten strings of red beads,
and ten pearl ones,
three baize aprons,
a spotted girdle,
a flaxen woof,
nine balls of thread,
seven unbleached linen hand towels,
fourteen milking cows with a feeding bag.

Olya listened, never missed a word, and trunk after trunk opened up before her full to the top, and the last and the fourteenth one with cows.

"We went to milk them," Granny recalled, "and instead of milk there was blood. And when we began to search we caught a witch in a mortar, with long hair, in a white shift, just a young wench."

Sometimes Granny took out a carved jewel casket and showed Olya her jewels.

Olya liked best a chain of gold rings with emeralds, but better still—she would have liked to put it round her neck immediately!—a gold heart-shaped medallion with a picture: two terrible lions with wide-flung jaws and flame coming out.

And each time Olya begged to be given both the emerald chain and the medallion with the terrible lions.

But Granny put the jewels back in the box.

"When you grow up big," Granny said, "Daddy will give you all the things, it will all be yours. Take as good care of the medallion as of your own eyes, there is no other like it, it's the Il'menevs' family medallion with Daddy's crest: lion's head, grey-maned with fiery jaw, on a field azure."

"Lion's head, grey-maned with fiery jaw, on a field azure," Olya repeated each time.

Once one of Granny's teeth fell out.

And Olya wanted to play with the tooth, she started throwing it from hand to hand and twisting it about, like a little top.

"I shall want the tooth to be put in my coffin," Granny stopped her, "so that when I rise again I won't have to crawl long over the ground searching for my bones. Everything must be together."

II

In the evenings Natalya Ivanovna used to play the piano and she played so well: Olya sat motionless, just listening. And when she finished playing, Olya would come up to the piano and drag a whole mountain of music on to the stool, and then she would settle down and begin to play herself.

"Olya will be a musician!" Natalya Ivanovna said of her.

After dinner Olya went to Granny's room as usual to ask about the rabbit, but Granny didn't answer and didn't give her any sweets. Olya understood that Granny wasn't well and didn't trouble her.

And in the evening she didn't go to ask Granny about the rabbit, but sat down at the piano to pick out the keys with her fingers and became so engrossed that she even forgot all about the rabbit.

And suddenly Granny appeared on the threshold of the ballroom——

Granny crept up to the door and spoke in such a quiet muted voice that Olya's fingers trembled:

"Olya, fetch Daddy!"

For a long time afterwards Olya was afraid of the door through which Granny had crept.

And how frightened she had been then! How her heart had frozen and thumped!

The day before, the children had been taken to a party at the Lupechevs—the Lupechevs had a party each year on the Day of St. Peter and St. Paul, they celebrated the birthday and saints-day of their twin sons, Peter and Paul—Olya had gone to bed late the night before, but she couldn't sleep the next night.

She kept seeing things: Grandfather Paul Petrovich the same as in his portrait in a red uniform walking about with a knife, or a witch with long hair in a white shift just a wench would come running into the yard and do something with her hands on the mortar, or a trunk with fourteen milking cows coming out of it—sticking out their horns, or the rabbit with sweets would flash past and after the rabbit, the lion's head, grey-maned with fiery jaw, on a field azure, and again as that evening, Granny would come creeping to the door and say in a quiet muted voice:

"Olya, fetch Daddy."

And she dreamed a bad dream.

She dreamt she was walking to the pond in spring and a péasant stood in the tall grass by the reeds, a scythe on his shoulder, all shaggy, with a white spot in one eye. And it seemed to Olya as if the peasant would fling himself at her from the long grass the very next moment with his scythe——

And then she woke in a fright.

And afterwards she could hardly fall asleep again; she kept being frightened, kept seeing the peasant, the scythe on his shoulder, his eye with a white spot.

And just as soon as dawn broke her father woke Olya and led her to Granny's room. Irena, Lena and Misha were all there and Vatagino's Father Evdokim with the deacon.

Granny sat up white in bed, all in white, holding a candle in her hands.

"Kiss Granny's hand, Olya!" her father said.

Granny made the sign of the cross over Olya with a trembling hand.

Alexander Pavlovich sat next to Granny on the bed, and holding up the candle in her hand, said:

"Into Thy hands, O Lord, I give my soul!"

III

In the middle of the day when the children were in the midst of their favourite game—making little Easter cakes out of sand—they were told to come in from the garden and were led into the ballroom—— .

"To bow to your Granny who has died."

All in white Granny was laid out upon a table standing slantwise away from the mantelpiece with its figured bronze clock and opposite the Il'menevs' miracle-working ikon of the Mother of God: a cross in her hands, her face covered with muslin.

The flies settled on Granny's hands and on her face.

Nurse Fatevna was driving the flies away.

In the spring when her youngest sister, Tanya, died, Olya couldn't understand it and kept asking: how is it that Granny is old and she is alive and Tanya is little and has died ?

"And so now Granny's turn has come," Olya decided, "only Granny is lying in a white dress and not in a little blue one like Tanya, and there are no coins on her eyes and they put coins on Tanya's!"

A swift golden sunbeam ran over Granny and played on the cross and on the halo and only at sunset did it suddenly hop away on to the mantelpiece, flash into the figured bronze clock and not show itself any more.

Nurse Fatevna put all Granny's teeth beneath her head and set a glass of water at her head.

"So that Granny's soul may bathe itself," the old nurse explained to Olya.

Olya did not take her eyes off the glass—bubbles rose in the glass—and Olya imagined Granny's soul bathing.

"Diving in the glass!"

A great many people came to Vatagino and the Il'menevs' house was full, all the rooms were occupied.

Their favourite Granny, Tatiana Alexeyevna, came from Mezheninka, and Uncle Alexey Ivanovich from town—he was Natalya Ivanovna's brother, a doctor—their aunts came, Alexander Pavlovich's sisters, Lyudmila Pavlovna and Nadezhda Pavlovna, and their neighbours the Borovs, the Lupechevs, the Sakhnovskys, the Graches, and the queer old man from Lubenetzi, Ksaverii Matveevich with Alexandrina Kensorinovna and their "Apostles," as that eccentric gentleman called his oxen, and friends and relations whom Olya had not set eyes on or heard anything of from the day she was born.

And they carried Granny off to church.

They tolled the bell all the way: that sound—it seemed to cry, yet one could listen to it for ever, it caught at one's heart so.

They laid Granny down in the middle of the church and went away.

And they locked the church door.

Olya kept worrying and asking they should bury Granny quickly in her grave——

"Granny will be frightened alone all night in the empty church."

Next day they buried Granny.

Olya cried: she was so sorry for Granny.

"Don't cry, Olyushka," Nurse Fatevna comforted her,

"you're sure to see Granny again, when you die too, your turn
will come and Granny will be happy to see you. And meanwhile
Granny will pray to God for you."

Olya grew calm and stopped crying.

"Why aren't you crying?" Nurse Fatevna would remark,
"be sure and cry a little, Olyushka! Or Granny's soul will see
that you are not crying and will think you are not sorry and will
be sad."

And Olya cried and tried not to let her attention wander.

They buried Granny next to Grandfather by the church—
in the graveyard where there were many crosses—cross by cross
—the Il'menevs' crosses.

IV

Granny was not there any more. Her room was empty.

The rabbit didn't come any more and bring sweets.

The table on which Granny had lain white, all in white, was
not there any more either. And the mirror above the mantelpiece was covered in white.

The lamp burned before the Il'menevs' miracle-working ikon
of the Mother of God and the figured bronze clock ticked on the
mantelpiece.

"On the day of Granny's death," Nurse Fatevna related,
"Granny had a dream, a girl came into her room, a white handkerchief in her hands; and Granny knew that this girl had come
to bear away her soul in the white handkerchief."

"Anyone may die at any moment," her father told Olya.

And Olya was frightened of death——

The turn will come, the girl will come, a white handkerchief
in her hands; and all the rooms, all the wings—the whole house
will become empty."

Granny Anna Mikhailovna was old, she never left her room,
always sat up in bed, and Nurse Fatevna was older still, although
she went on a pilgrimage every summer.

Olya paid heed to Nurse Fatevna; they said Fatevna *knew everything*.

On Saturdays Nurse Fatevna bathed the children.

When she shampooed Olya's hair she always told her something; she told how she herself had not washed her hair for sixty years——

"Because you should not wash your hair after you have been married—it's sinful for a married woman to remain with her hair uncovered even for an hour."

And she said she had lived for a long time and would live for a long time yet because she had honoured and obeyed her father and mother.

"And you, Olya," said Nurse Fatevna, "won't live so long: you don't do as Mummy tells you, you keep running off to the windmill."

"This is the seventh year I have lived in this world of ours!" Olya announced and rubbing her soapy eyes with her small fists, she said, interrupting: "and the rabbit who brought Granny sweets, is he dead too?"

CHAPTER TWO

I

WHEN Olya settled down on the Il'menevs' old couch, the Consoler, her legs did not reach the edge by a long way and another person could easily find room on it, she was so small still.

Olya did not like dolls, and if anyone gave her a doll for a present she would give it to the other children and not play with it herself.

She gave all her love to all manner of little knick-knacks, all sorts of different little cups, little boxes and tiny caskets—and she played with them instead of dolls: she hid them, moved them from place to place, treasured them.

Olya kept these treasures safe in a big black casket—her favourite Granny had given it her!   And in this casket she put all her presents—boxes of sweets, which were taken from her when she wasn't looking—and Olya didn't guess, she didn't notice!—and into the same casket at Shrovetide Olya put some pancakes, so that her pancakes would lie there too——

"All together!"

And Olya had some special favourites from which she could seldom be parted, which she kept carrying round with her, her favourites.

II

Olya went out to visit their neighbours, she came back home and oh, she found she hadn't got her favourite little casket—it wasn't there, she'd forgotten it!—and at once she got ready to go and fetch it back.

Her little casket was over there, she knew it, she would run back quickly for it, and again it would be with her, her tiny little casket.

And Olya had already run down the steps of the porch to cross the yard, when——

A dog had got into the yard, not just any dog, but a mad dog, a rabid dog!—and a tumult arose in the yard, everyone rushed about in a fright: the children were taken into the house and Nurse Fatevna dragged Olya after her indoors.

They shut the windows as they did when a storm was approaching.

And all the doors were shut.

The dogs wailed fearfully in the yard.

It was fearful in the yard, frightening even to look.

Dogs from all quarters came running into the yard at the sound of the wailing and the mad dog was dealing with them: the mad dog was *mangling* the others—it threw itself at them and tore them with its teeth—it would roll a dog over on the ground and tear it as it lay there, till the fur flew!

The dogs skated about like tops, fell head over heels, shrieked from the maddening pain, shrieked in frothing, tearing shrieks!

The mad wailing and shrieking hung over the yard.

There was no question of going into the yard, of showing your nose there even—you would hardly find anyone venturing out of the house even if bent on the most important business!

Men had been sent to the village to fetch some *muzhiks* and now they were expected any minute: *muzhiks* would come with stakes and finish the dog off.

But what was to be done, how could Olya stay apart from her favourite little casket for so long ?

She didn't want to wait—she wanted it now!

And Olya started to cry, and how she cried——

Olya was like that: if she wanted anything she must have it at once!—she would lie on the floor and beat her legs and arms against the floor—please give it her!

The Il'menevs had visitors.

And everyone did his best to persuade and comfort Olya; they kept telling her about the *muzhiks* who would come with stakes and then she could go where she liked, whilst now no one could go for her little casket, no one would agree to go, all the servants and hands had hidden away.

"Can't!"

"Impossible!"

But Olya didn't want to listen: she beat upon the floor, cried, and how she cried!—give, O give her, her little casket, get it at once——

"My little casket!"

And at last Alexander Pavlovich, Olya's father—he loved Olya so much!—took a stick, picked Olya up from the floor in his arms—Olya clasped him round the neck, where had all her tears gone now!—and he left the room with her, opened the door, went out on to the porch and straight into the yard——

And immediately the mad dog left the others and threw itself upon him.

III

The way from the porch to the gate seemed terribly long to Olya, as long as from the porch to church, no, even longer, as long as from the porch to the windmill.

Olya was very, very frightened.

Her father kept the dog off with his stick, threw it off and went on—he pushed the stick into its throat, thrust it right down its throat.

The dog gasped for breath, fell back and then suddenly rushed forward again and more furiously and ragingly than ever.

Olya clutched her father round the neck more and more tightly from fear, she squeezed him with her small hands so tightly that he couldn't shout at the dog any more—Olya was throttling him.

But she didn't guess—she didn't notice! Olya thought: "Daddy isn't afraid and only Olya is frightened!"

The long way from the porch to the wicket-gate came to an end—Alexander Pavlovich carried Olya beyond the gates.

And soon she had her favourite little casket in her hands again.

And meanwhile the *muzhiks* came hurrying up: they took their sticks to the mad dog——.

CHAPTER THREE

I

OLYA wrote well: she didn't make mistakes.

Olya always had full marks for Russian.

Her teacher, Natalya Vasil'evna, liked Olya because she always got her spelling right.

And why did she get her spelling right?

Olya set herself this question and invented explanations—and one reason seemed the most likely.

When she was still very small, Olya would not be able to get to sleep sometimes; she would lie in bed at night, awake, and to amuse herself she divided words up into syllables——

> ko-ro-va
> ta-rel-ka
> med-ved'*

"I expect I divided every single word up into syllables then in the night and that's why I spell every word right now."

And Olya would notice mistakes in anyone's writing.

Yet she was still only in the third form.

She was eleven years old.

II

The holidays were drawing near—it was Christmas time.

Olya was longing to go home: she was lodging in town but her thoughts were all over there in Vatagino.

Olya was waiting for someone to come and fetch her.

But no, Natasha Grigor'evna's brother came for her and the Grigor'evs lived only three versts from them, so Olya had a letter from her mother.

Natalya Ivanovna wrote that Yuri Vasil'evitch Grigor'ev would take Olya to Vatagino: she had asked him to do this.

Olya read the letter and noticed it had two mistakes.

"Two mistakes!"

Next morning Olya went to the High School to ask for her return ticket home.

But the headmistress gave her no ticket—she didn't want to let her go back home.

"I can't let you go with a strange young man! If you could give me some assurance such as a letter from your mother or your father that they allowed you to travel with him, then I would let you go."

And Olya's spirits fell.

---

* In Russian:—cow—plate—bear.   *Translator's Note.*

The letter lay in her pocket: if she produced it, the head-mistress would at once give her leave and she would be home tomorrow—just in time.

"But Mummy's letter has two spelling mistakes! The head-mistress will notice that my mother has made two mistakes. No, not for anything!"

So she didn't show the letter.

And she was left without her holiday.

Olya returned to her boarding establishment—everyone was going home: a father came for one, a mother for another, a third had a letter.

Olya alone was left.

And Olya wept all day and all night and all the next day and night.

On Christmas Eve Olya's Aunt, Marya Petrovna came and took Olya to her house: she had only just heard that they had not allowed Olya to go home.

And Olya cried away a whole day at her Aunt's: her eyes got red with weeping, and swollen, and her nose got red and swollen too.

But she kept crying.

"Well, but why didn't you show your letter?" Marya Pe-trovna said in agitation.

"It—had—two mistakes."

And again as soon as she remembered their house—the Christmas tree lit up . . . their favourite Granny telling about the Magi, how the Magi travelled with the star, and each time it seemed to Olya that there were many Magi and all women, bear-ing the star in their hands and the star guiding them with its light!—as soon as she remembered she burst into tears.

III

On Christmas morning Alexander Pavlovich arrived: he had ridden post all night from Vatagino.

Olya flung herself into his arms—how near to her it all was, the heavy uniform coat of Nicholas I's reign, and her father's grey hair, which she could hardly reach as she jumped, and his eyes!—Olya squealed with joy!

Well, now they could go.

Without waiting for dinner they set off home.

Olya did not feel very well on the way—she couldn't stand the motion of the sledge!—she got worn out.

And towards the end it rocked her to sleep.

She woke because the horses had neighed loudly.

They were at the porch already.

In the window the Christmas tree blazed——

And in the porch stood Natalya Ivanovna, their favourite Granny, Nurse Fatevna—they were all standing waiting for Olya.

Olya jumped out—and there was another treat for her!—she asked for tea and tea was standing all ready with lemon jam.

"Mummy guessed what happened to me on the journey!" Olya drank tea from her favourite cup with lemon jam.

And the children from the neighbouring house came.

They ran playing about the Christmas tree a long time.

They were given a great many sweets and dainties.

But they made their favourite ones themselves: they burnt sugar over a candle and the result was toffees—they loved doing this and were only given permission very rarely—but what delicious toffees they were!

Olya's father, her mother and her granny made the sign of the cross over her when she went to bed.

Her father said:

"Christ be with you!"

Her mother said:

"May your guardian angel shield you!"

And Granny whispered:

"Blessed be the Lord!"

And when Olya lay in bed under her favourite blanket, Nurse Fatevna was poking about in all the corners for something:

"We must light all the ikon lamps. Today the unclean spirit is malevolent: he is angered that Christ is born."

And in the porch stood Natalya Ivanovna, their favourite Granny, Nurse Fatevna.

And as she passed she too made the sign of the cross over Olya.

And Olya fell fast asleep, intoning a happy song in her nose.

CHAPTER FOUR

I

OLYA'S plait was rather a big one with a blue ribbon.

If you were to ask her what she loved best, Olya would answer:

"Easter time."

She counted her days from one Easter to the next.

When a cake was put in the oven, Olya lay down and cried a little into her pillow—you should cry a bit like that to make sure the cake would be a success.

When the Easter yeast cakes were rising, Olya didn't move from room to room, because a noise was bad for the cake—you could go barefoot but only if it was absolutely unavoidable.

The Easter cakes were a source of great anxiety: if they were not a success, if they had a hollow inside them, you could be sure that that year someone in the house would die—you had to have your wits about you with Easter cakes!

Olya took part wholeheartedly in everything which was done—in all the paschal preparations.

Olya watched old Nurse Fatevna knead the dough before setting it in the oven: how she seized it deftly from the kneading-trough and threw it on the board, she would throw it once, then a second time and then a third—even dough obeyed Fatevna!

Olya helped them to arrange the freshly baked Easter cakes on cushions—you had to put fresh Easter cakes on cushions!

She made pretty paper frills for the fancy cakes.

And she did a whole lot of other things which had to be done for such a red-letter day, the day from which Olya counted all her days.

One thing she couldn't get the knack of—Olya couldn't separate the whites from the yolks.

And Olya was not allowed to cream the cream cheese for the *paskhi* with a wooden spoon in the mixing bowl: the Easter before she had stirred and stirred till the bottom of the bowl fell out.

"I told you too many cooks spoil the broth!" Nurse Fatevna had said on that occasion.

But in time Olya would achieve wisdom in this too—she was capable and a good little girl.

II

It was Palm Sunday.

Another day or two and they would break up for Easter.

Olya had a letter from home: both her father and her mother wrote to say that Olya would not be able to come home to Vatagino.

"The road is cut off—a big flood has burst the river—it's impossible to travel!"

Olya was very upset: she had never spent Easter in town and she couldn't imagine what kind of an Easter they had there! —she knew and loved her Vatagino Easter, awaited it eagerly, thought of it all the time.

As soon as Passion Week began, the days of the week would fly by in a kind of fever.

And on Easter Eve such a fuss and palaver began that everything was topsy-turvy: if you had time for a bite—well and good, if not—blame yourself!—everyone was up to the eyes in work.

And at last the Saturday evening came.

All the children were put to bed until eleven, and at eleven precisely Nurse Fatevna woke them all: it was time to get ready for the midnight service.

When Olya walked through the ballroom in her white party dress with a blue ribbon, she was afraid——

In the corner before the Il'menevs' miracle-working ikon a

little lamp was burning—one solitary lamp was lighting the huge ballroom.

In the middle of the room, stretching from the piano to the mantelpiece with its figured bronze clock, stood a white table decked with flowers.

On the table stood all the Easter cakes and the *paskhi*:

> a white *paskha*,[*]
> a brown *paskha*,
> a large *paskha*,
> a little *paskha*,
> a smaller one still;

and all the big cakes:

> a sand cake,
> a butter cake,
> a fruit cake,
> a chocolate cake,
> a rye cake,
> an almond cake;

and a bristling ham,
and a turkey, stuffed with almonds and white cereal,
and a leg of veal;
wines, and liqueurs:

> rose,
> gooseberry,
> barberry,
> yellow plum brandy,
> red plum brandy,

and, finally—a sucking piglet.

Olya was afraid of the piglet.

As soon as she entered the room her eyes always fell upon the piglet first: the piglet lay importantly on a large dish right under the chandelier and he held a horseradish in his mouth.

---

* A rich Easter sweetmeat made from a kind of cream cheese with cream, sugar, eggs and butter. The mixture is put in a pyramid-shaped mould under a weight till it becomes firm. It is eaten with *kulich*, a cake made with yeast.
                                                            Translator's Note.

Olya couldn't say herself why she was afraid of the piglet, but every Easter as she passed through the ballroom she was afraid just of him: he lay on the dish with a horseradish in his mouth.

The whole household set off on foot for church—you couldn't ride that night: Gregory the coachman went ahead with the lantern and Misha and Lena went with him, then Natalya Ivanovna with Irena, then the butler, Fedot the Bent, and the valet, Fedot the Straight, after the Fedots Nurse Fatevna with a little bundle, and far in front—in front of everyone, Olya and Alexander Pavlovich with her.

And all the way her heart grew still with suspense:

"Suppose it's not the same this year?" Olya thought, "suppose they don't sing 'Christ is Risen'?"

Old women sat by the church—their heads covered with long white shawls, like shrouds.

And there were Easter cakes and *paskhi* and piglets, all brought to church to be blessed, lying covered with white muslin, by the old women.

Olya remembered how once her father had told her and Nurse Fatevna too more than once, that on Easter Eve the dead rise from their graves.

Olya gazed intently at the old women——

Why, these were not old women at all but dead people who were buried in the churchyard, sitting here by the church!

And Olya wanted to look more closely and her eyes flickered with fear.

In the procession behind the cross, Olya went next to Vatagino's Father Evdokim, and behind him with the people, with all the villagers and the womenfolk, the dead came too, the buried, with the late Anna Mikhailovna, their Granny, and Sister Tanya who died.

Olya knew it, she could hear them—she felt their steps behind—there were many of them in white shrouds and the old were all in white, the little ones in blue dresses like Tanya——

And her heart thumped.

When the procession of the Cross passed Granny's grave, Olya's candle was like her heart—and in the swaying candlelight she saw that Granny's grave was standing open.

They had a custom in Vatagino: the Il'menevs' coachman Gregory used to impersonate the devil on Easter Eve.

He stayed alone in the church during the procession of the Cross, and, standing by the door, he leant on it with all his might and main to prevent the procession from getting back into the church. But immediately Father Evdokim said on the threshold: "The Lord shall rise again" and behind him they began to sing the "Christ is Risen!" for the first time, the devil could hold out no longer, he lost his strength, shrivelled, rushed headlong across the church and escaped out through some chink——

The church door opened wide and with the candlelight the singing voices poured within:

"Christ is Risen!"

Olya wept, without noticing her tears, she saw such a bright joyous light, she felt this light about her, heart and soul, enveloping her, and she couldn't not cry——

"Christ is Risen!"

"Olyushka," Nurse whispered in her ear, "how bright your face is; Olyushka, Christ is risen!"[*]

They would stand through matins and then go home.

In front went Gregory the coachman with a lantern, and Misha and Lena after him, then Natalya Ivanovna with Irena, then the butler, Fedot the Bent, and the valet, Fedot the Straight, and after the Fedots, after everyone else, Nurse Fatevna with her bundle.

And Olya and her father were far ahead again.

And they passed a great many villagers and their womenfolk—with Easter cakes, *paskhi* and piglets.

As soon as dawn glimmered little lights burnt in the cottages.

---

[*] After midnight has struck on Easter Eve people greet each other: "Christ is Risen!"
"Risen indeed!" and exchange three kisses on either cheek.
Translator's Note.

"And how is it he doesn't burst!" thought Olya.

At home they waited for Father Evdokim—the whole house was lit up—they waited and waited.

And at last Father Evdokim arrived, blessed the *paskhi* and exchanged the Easter greeting with them all.

But Olya had long ago kissed not only all the servants but all the hands on the estate too, and the flowers and her favourite little boxes, all her books, except—her Geography book—that wasn't a favourite.

Father Evdokim cut himself a little piece of Easter cake and of *paskha* and then everyone could eat—then they broke the fast.

"And how is it he doesn't burst!" thought Olya, gazing at Father Evdokim, who had to taste everything first, not only at their house, but at all their neighbours': at the Borovs' and the Lupechevs' and the Sakhnovskys' and the Grigor'evs' and even in Lubenetzi, at the house of the queer old man Ksaverii Matveevich.

And how merrily the first day of Easter passed!

It was good to swing on Easter Day, to leap on boards of wood, to roll eggs——

The church bells rang all day.

* * * * *

Olya knew she lived for Easter Night and Easter Day alone.

And how could Olya possibly not be in Vatagino that night? How could she possibly remain there in town, in the boarding establishment, where everything had got so dull after a whole winter?

No, Olya was sure, she kept telling herself over and over—she would go home for certain.

And she would be so happy, so happy that she would even kiss her Geography book.

Palm Sunday went by, the first three days went by—the Monday, Tuesday and Wednesday of Passion Week—Olya fasted and received Holy Communion—Good Friday went by too.

No one came for Olya.

And then when it looked as if no hope remained, on Easter Eve the Il'menevs' neighbour, Sakhnovsky, arrived in the morning, called at the Linde *pension* and they let Olya go home with him.

Everything was ready and the table set when Olya arrived in Vatagino.

And it only remained for her to make sure that everything was right: that the eggs were coloured right and what Easter cakes there were and what *paskhi*, and what the piglet was like.

"You didn't expect you would get home for Easter?"

"No, Mummy, I was sure I should come."

"The heart knows best and you can't deceive it with words or with letters!" Alexander Pavlovich said, gazing at his grey-eyed daughter.

And when night came everything happened as it had always happened.

As in former years, Olya got frightened of the piglet when she crossed the ballroom, and on the way to church was very worried that they would not sing the "Christ is Risen," she saw the dead by the church, and in the swaying of the candle among the procession of the Cross she saw her Granny's grave standing open, and again when they sang "Christ is Risen!" for the first time she wept for joy and Nurse Fatevna whispered:

"Olyushka, how bright your face is; Olyushka, Christ is Risen!"

Olya decided that whatever happened she would not miss the sunrise. Nurse Fatevna told her that on Easter Day the sun rose differently from usual:

"You can see plainly in the sun how Christ rises from the grave, or how Christ ascends into heaven, or just a cross emerging from the sun."

And when they had broken their fast and Father Evdokim had gone away, and the whole house had gone to bed, Olya went up into the tower where the library was and sat down by the window to wait for the sun.

And the sun rose——

red——

gold——

the whole garden flamed and all the birds began to sing.

The sun rose above the house, and stopped directly opposite the tower—Olya's eyes were dazzled.

And Olya didn't see anything.

Olya went to nurse and she woke Nurse Fatevna up.

"What does it mean, I didn't see anything in the sun?"

"I expect you screwed up your eyes at the very moment it happened," her old nurse said, "but I saw Christ rising from the grave, Olyushka."

Olya believed Fatevna.

"Christ rose from the grave!"

And she wasn't sad for long.

Next time she would gaze with all her eyes and see it! Even if her tears rained down she wouldn't blink or screw up her eyes!—she would see everything.

CHAPTER FIVE

I

OLYA was a tomboy with the best, you felt she couldn't sit still for a single moment, she'd spread her wings and begin to shout and run in circles round the hall—nothing would stop her, she'd get the whole school on their feet.

She could be angry too.

"When I'm angry I get like my dress!" Olya herself had said more than once, before she went to school, and she would point at her favourite red flannel dress with black spots, "that's what I'm like!"

The most popular master was Yakov Stepanovich Theophilactov, a physicist, who taught the IVth form geography—it was a custom they had in the Pokidosh High School to make the teacher of physics take geography as well.

And Yakov Stepanovich took Geography.

The IVth form were doing Russia.

Giving preference to provincial towns, Yakov Stepanovich tackled all the rest of the geography without any elaborate plan —simply: he recounted the adventures which befell him when he was walking all over Russia with his friend——

——and his friend knew everything whilst he himself knew nothing.

Each time, whatever was being explained, this friend who knew everything would appear.

Once they were travelling along impenetrable marshlands and Yakov Stepanovich sank up to his knees in a bog and so awkwardly that he couldn't clamber out in any way, whilst his friend who knew everything, as luck would have it, had disappeared somewhere. And another time, all because of a wretched bit of a match, lighting a camp-fire on the outskirts of a wood, they burnt down a dense and ancient forest, and Yakov Stepanovich himself only escaped by hiding under a sorrel bush of some sort and then only by luck.

It was all in this style—lively, graphic, amusing.

Either because of the stories about his friend or because someone accused Yakov Stepanovich of saying in the heat of his reminiscences at a lesson with the IVth form:

That man is descended from monkeys!

But for some time past the headmistress and the director had taken to attending the geography lessons.

On such invasions Yakov Stepanovich without any embarrassment called up the worst pupils and that was as far as the lesson went, no stories were told, and only the same homework set for next time. So the heads went away without anything to go on.

Olya's favourite possession was her little globe which she used to put away carefully with all her small boxes and towards which she felt a special tenderness, but Olya didn't like geography and when it was her turn to answer questions, she rattled off whatever came into her head quite at random, only briskly and boldly.

"That's it, bear that in mind!" Yakov Stepanovich would approve.

And it was not only for things like this that Yakov Stepanovich was popular.

"Just try telling another master you haven't prepared your lesson and he'll give you 'one' and turn you out of the class like a shot, but Yakov Stepanovich never does that, if only you admit it quite truthfully and straight out."

And it was true, explanations like the following often took place at geography lessons.

A girl had not learnt her lesson:

"Why not?"

"I went for a drive."

"Where did you go?"

"Beyond the Kiev Bridge."

"How is the road now? I haven't been for a drive for a long while, you know!" Yakov Stepanovich stretched himself luxuriously: he was very fond of a drive. "Whom did you go with?"

"With a friend."

"Now that's what I like: you went driving—what's the harm in it, if you went driving, you went driving. But as for these headaches, toothaches, excuses like that!"

But in the Pokidosh High School where the form mistresses kept a look-out in the streets, if the head got to know you'd been out driving and with a boy, you'd get a "three" for conduct or even get expelled!

With what enjoyment Yakov Stepanovich would yawn! And he yawned most luxuriously at the most inappropriate times—at exams and in front of the heads when it felt as if even the desks the walls and the table and the ceiling were in a flutter.

He was so lanky that he stooped, with curly sandy red hair to his shoulders, and a nose cleft at the tip almost as if there were two grown together, and his top lip—however you looked at it you couldn't see anything above this lip, as if there was nothing there and never had been.

Yakov Stepanovich fell in love with the mistress of the preparatory class, Faina Alexandrovna Gromov.

This had been remarked on long ago and was stale news to them all. They waited eagerly for the *dénouement*, fixed on a date for the wedding themselves, and were getting ready to congratulate him in class, when suddenly Yakov Stepanovich announced:

"Today I'm giving you my last lesson, or the last but one. I'm going away."

"What?" the class cried.

"I'm going away."

"Stay!" they shouted. "Don't go away, Yakov Stepanovich!"

"No, I can't." Yakov Stepanovich rumpled up his hair and propped his brow on his fists so that not only his eyes, but even his nose, cleft at the tip, was hidden, and only his one lip and his red beard stuck out in a tuft. "I can't, a man cannot remain in some places if he is misunderstood and rejected."

"Do stay! We understand you," the girls cried.

It was quite clear: of course Yakov Stepanovich had proposed to Faina Alexandrovna and been refused.

"No, I can't, I'm going away," Yakov Stepanovich insisted.

"Don't go, stay, don't go!" the class roared and wailed, and you couldn't make out whether they were pretending or quite in earnest.

"I'm sorry, I can't stay even for you, I'm sorry!"

And he just went off—for a whole month they saw absolutely nothing of him. In a month's time he reappeared and seemed so happy, his dark blue eyes shining.

"Girls, I'm staying."

And there was no secret about it; everyone guessed: of course, Yakov Stepanovich was going to marry Faina Alexandrovna. And a lot of lessons went by in conversations like these.

Yakov Stepanovich used to walk about the classroom, on and on, and if he found an empty desk he would sit down.

When Yakov Stepanovich sat in front of Olya she would begin teasing him: she quietly caught one of his hairs on her pencil, wound it round and gave it a jerk.

Poor Yakov Stepanovich would scratch his head and if you looked next day you could see his hair was all fluffed up—he'd washed it! That meant he'd thought a flea was responsible!

* * * * *

The most frightening master was Philemon Petrovich Kurapov, the historian.

No tricks or dodges got you anywhere.

One of the girls tried to stage a fainting fit—he merely got up from his chair.

"Stop pretending, go to your place!" that was all.

So she just went.

And what juicy "ones" with moustaches he gave, written full in the square!—You couldn't scratch them out with a penknife, and all for the merest trifles.

One called Pope Leo X: "Pope Leus X."

"One."

Another said that in the Turkish War peace was concluded at:

"Stefan Batory."

"One."

A third, telling about Julius Caesar, didn't make a pause in the correct place:

"In the midst of the conspirators," the girl stated, "Julius Caesar saw Brutus who had received so many benefits at his hands, cried: 'You too, Brutus, wrapped his toga about him and fell dead at the foot of the statue of Pompey'."

"One."

When Philemon Petrovich had finished explaining the lesson, he patted his grey tufts of hair in place and disappeared behind a journal, and then a chill would run through the class and such a silence fall that you could not only hear a fly but the tiniest most invisible little insect, and in this terrible moment Olya would puff out her cheeks and slap them with her fists.

And if you knocked the table to bits tapping it with your pencil—Philemon Petrovich always tapped the table with his

pencil on such occasions—you still couldn't find out where this
noise came from.

* * * * *

Olya learnt well.   She was intelligent.

She had no need of anyone else's wits.

When her younger sister Lena was being weaned (Lena was
three years younger than Olya) Olya heard her granny telling her
mother to put a mixture of honey and mustard on her breasts,
and she brought Lena a little rag so that she could wipe them:

"Otherwise it'll taste bitter."

She could parse sensibly, tell a story sensibly—Olya remembered everything, she never had to struggle to learn by heart, it
came easily to her, she did her dictations without mistakes and
could solve any problem set.

The terror of the school—the arithmetic mistress, Katerina
Feodorovna was satisfied with Olya.

And Katerina Feodorovna, who doled out not only "ones"
and "twos" freely, but also notabenes she made up, was no fool
at setting problems: for instance, she would make you solve a
problem not just normally but from the end—you try.

But Olya could solve it backwards too: she went through all
the points in the solution briskly, and not from the first as one
usually did, but from the very last to the first, that was the whole
secret of it.

But still before she went up from the IInd to the IIIrd form
Olya was re-examined in arithmetic.

It was like this.   The inspector came and asked for the best
pupil to be called forward.   Olya was chosen.   But Olya did not
know a thing: she had been questioned the day before, and had
not glanced at her book since or listened to the explanation in
class.   Katerina Feodorovna gave her "one."   And at the exam
she set Olya such a problem—there was no general problem—
that Olya sat solving it and solving it, gave in her last notebook
and still hadn't got any answer.   She was given a *viva*.   And she
had the same problem at the re-examination, and again had
"two" for it.   So she was made to take the exam again.   And

no one to whom Olya took her problem could solve it. The problem was quite simply insoluble: there are some like that in the exercise books.

"We have a private account to settle," Katerina Feodorovna explained to the teacher who was present at Olya's second exam and who was very surprised that Olya had failed when he saw how well she seemed to know everything.

* * * * *

Olya wanted to learn. She had made a firm resolution when she was still in the IInd form to learn and to learn a lot.

Olya got a sore throat and Dr. Schreiber was attending to it—Olya had to see her once a week—and from the first time she went Olya was very taken with the little brass name-plate:

Doctor Freda Lazarevna Schreiber

From that time she dreamed of becoming a doctor.

And for that, as she found out, you had to study a great deal.

So she resolved firmly to learn and to learn a lot.

Only Olya was rather clumsy, she couldn't settle down: either she'd upset the inkwell, or spill some water, or stumble or bang herself and always in a place where anyone else would come through unscathed she would immediately get a bruise, or again, she'd burn her hand or knock her nose so that it bled. It was as though the ground couldn't hold her—you could expect an accident daily.

When Olya was quite small she nearly crippled herself for life.

One day the samovar was brought in and put on a stool and, as luck would have it, there was no one in the dining-room but Olya. She went up to the samovar and either pushed it or got herself caught in it so that it tipped over and fell straight on her: it scalded both her legs.

And when they started taking off her stockings the skin came away too.

What could you expect? It was lucky her legs escaped.

But that was not fatal—it might have been far worse.

Olya was always getting lost.

She would go for a walk with one of the grown-ups and invariably either lag behind or run on ahead and, of course, get lost. And she never knew where she was going, just wherever God willed, as if the wind were driving her. They'd realise she was gone, hunt and search for her, and then at last in some completely unexpected place—in a ravine, or in someone else's yard, or far off in the fields—they'd find her.

Once she found herself on the outskirts of the village near the hut of some Jews. She didn't know the way back, of course, and just sat down and cried. The Jews came out of their cottage, and began asking her to come in—she wouldn't come and cried all the harder.

She was very offended. Why did the Jews call her Lyuba? She was sure everyone knew her name.

She had a job getting home: the old Jew brought her back.

And sometimes Olya even managed to get lost in her own house: for instance, she'd wander off into some distant room— the Il'menevs' house was ancient, enormous, with nineteen rooms —and not be able to get back: the doors were heavy—they wouldn't obey her small hands, they'd shut all right, but open—no, they were too heavy, so she'd just scramble under a divan somewhere or under a bed and lie there, crying, till she was found.

"If you get lost in the street somewhere," Alexander Pavlovich explained to her one day, "just tell someone and you'll be brought back to me. Your surname is Il'menev."

From that time Olya knew what her surname was, and from that time she was not frightened of being lost.

"If I lose my way, I'll tell my surname and they'll bring me back to Daddy—everyone knows Daddy!" Olya worked it out like that, and when she lost herself she no longer wept but had her surname on the tip of her tongue for the first person she met.

Now in town she seemed to have got used to it a little, otherwise there was nothing you could do but hold her hand and never let go.

* * * * *

Olya could be very odd.

"Mummy, I can remember your wedding perfectly!" Olya said more than once.

And when Natalya Ivanovna explained to her that Olya couldn't possibly remember, she wasn't there and had only been born twelve years after the wedding, Olya would begin to argue: she brought up all sorts of details from the decoration of the room in which she had lain in swaddling clothes on the bed, the day of the wedding.

And it was true Olya had once lain in exactly such a room— here she was not inventing anything—but it was when she had been six weeks old and Natalya Ivanovna had taken her with her to a wedding on a neighbouring estate five versts from Vatagino.

Olya assured everyone that she was born on horseback and that Natalya Ivanovna was not her real mother, but her real mother was looking for her, and when Olya would be sixteen Olya would find her and she would find a friend for herself—a sister whose name she was sure would turn out to be Olya too.

"I was born on a saddle in a field and my real mother is looking for me," Olya would repeat.

Once it happened that Natalya Ivanovna went on a railway journey with Olya and Lena. During a halt Olya and Lena wanted to go on the platform for some water. Natalya Ivanovna gave them permission but then stopped Lena: Lena might fall down, let Olya go alone.

This hurt Olya terribly.

"Of course. I know you're not my real mother, my real mother wouldn't let me go, I might fall down too."

So they were left without water. Olya didn't want to go alone.

Olya very much wanted Natalya Ivanovna to be the real mother whom she would discover when she would be sixteen. That was why Olya liked sometimes to be a bit ill at home in Vatagino. Natalya Ivanovna became so kind then and loved her more than the others.

"Like a real mother!"

When Olya was well, Natalya Ivanovna loved her less—so it seemed to Olya—and she loved Irena most of all—Irena was six years older than Olya—because she was the oldest and because she was the most obedient and Natalya Ivanovna always made an example of her to Olya.

Olya was certainly an odd child and a very funny one, there was no doubt about it.

Look at the crazy thing she got up to when she was still quite tiny!

She started sitting on the floor: she'd settle herself down and sit quiet. They tried to get out of her why she went on sitting still. She wouldn't say a word in answer, just looked up slyly, and if she was picked up she started howling.

And then eventually it all came out: Olya had noticed, how to sleep the sounder, old Nurse Fatevna would undress, light a candle-end, and sticking her head under the collar of her shift would catch fleas with her candle; and Olya felt the urge, also to sleep the sounder, to catch a few fleas, and there were no fleas.

"If I sit on the floor," Olya decided, "and if I sit very still the fleas will come to me and I'll have a lot of fleas I can catch."

In her first period at school Olya learnt all her lessons every day, all the ones set and all the different subjects even if they were not down on the timetable, and she carried all her textbooks and exercise books in her satchel. All the texts and notebooks didn't fit in her satchel at once and Olya kneaded them in with her fists so that they soon got crumpled and torn. They soon came down on Olya for untidiness and the Russian mistress, Natalya Vasil'evna, gave her four instead of five at the end of term even though Olya was a favourite with her.

"For crumpled notebooks."

And what could you do?—it was a rule and the school was like that.

Not without good reason, after hearing the tales her eldest sister Irena told on coming home to Vatagino for the holidays from the Institute, Olya, then still only dreaming of the High School, imagined it precisely as strict and exacting as the Russian mistress made it, and she told Nurse Fatevna not without some pride:

"You know, Nurse, I'll go to school and at school they'll set a whole great fat book to be learnt by heart, and next day they'll make you answer, and if you leave out a 'but' you'll get 'two'!"

Once after the confessional to shorten the time—they weren't supposed to eat or drink—the girls were taken for a walk. Olya asked to call at a fruiterer's. Absolutely all she had was one rouble—this rouble was supposed to be set aside for the Father for communion. She took some apples in the shop and it turned out that they cost exactly one rouble, so she paid and was left with an empty pocket. Luckily the form mistress put matters right in time: the apples were returned and the rouble given back.

The first time Olya remained in town for Easter, she stood in the first couple in the High School church, and was the first to come up after matins to the priest at the cross—the Scripture master Aristotelev, and kept stretching up to kiss him the Easter greeting, but Father Aristotelev, considering it improper to kiss the schoolgirls even from the junior forms, turned away from the kiss and put forward the cross instead. Olya kissed the cross about ten times.

In the IInd form Olya cut off her eyebrows and was given "four" for conduct.

Well, wasn't she odd!

II

Olya entered the High School when she was nine, and was put in the Ist form. They had wanted to send her to the Institute but she had kicked up such a fuss that they were forced to give in willy-nilly, just as once before when Olya was five and had taken it into her head to go to confessional. The whole commotion arose only because they were taking her brother Misha—Misha was two years older than Olya—to the High School, and Olya insisted they should go together.

Olya was firm friends with her brother: sometimes they played at travellers for whole days on end, or built huts from planks of wood under the plum tree together, they were taught together by the same teacher, Ivan Il'ich. How could she help kicking up a fuss then ?

Just before Olya was taken away to the High School she ran round the whole house, the whole garden and the whole yard, saying good-bye to every corner in the house, the garden and the yard.

In the drawing-room and the sitting-room, the study and the portrait gallery she said good-bye to the portraits: to the purple eagle-eyed figure called "The Mighty" and the dusky brown picture called "Stormy Nights" and to the proud red Polish lady of the Gedroitz line of Hetmans and to the white Polish lady, delicate as feather-grass, from the warrior line of Gastol'da and to all the ladies and cavaliers, to all her ancestors, old and young, in brocade, in sable with staffs of office, in velvet, bepowdered, in silks, with such merry and beautiful faces and such frowning and terrible faces, and to her grandfather in his red uniform.

In the garden Olya said good-bye to the unfinished huts, to the fishpond and the other pond, to the old limes, the apple trees, the pear trees, the acacias beneath which her grandfather had played when he was small, and to all the arbours especially the "Philosophic Arbour," where an echo dwelt and if you called it would mimic you absolutely exactly, to the orange-houses and the statues and her favourite flowers: to the "Little-coal-in-the-fire," to the "Dishevelled Ladies," to the asters, the double-petalled hollyhocks and the roses.

In the stables she said good-bye to all the horses, in the sheds to the cattle, in the poultry-yards to the fowls, in the wood pile to the wood, where she liked to sit in the evening under the silver black poplar, in the coachhouse and the penthouses to the implements and the carriages: to Woebegone and Demonpush, to the charabancs, and to Bouncer and Trundleteer which could hold about twenty people—she glanced on to the roof of the shed where the stork stood on one leg guarding Olya's happiness;

Cadeau, the red hunter, turned up, she said good-bye to him and to all the dogs of the yard, to the black ones and the white ones.

"Good-bye," Olya said, panting, "your Olya is going away to school."

And it seemed to her they all replied:

"Good-bye, Olya, come back soon."

"I'll come back, I'll return a High School girl with a brown dress and a black apron."

She ran out of the gates to the church to the graveyard and her grandmother's grave, and from the graveyard back through the strawberries to the barn—waggons of corn were dragging their way into the barn, the threshing-machine rattled, she took great handfuls of grain, stood in the yard opposite the white-towered house, gazed round far into the distance, flung the grain high—and golden in the sunset like gold bees, they rose to the sky and fell upon Olya in a blue rain.

It seemed as if the stove itself and the walls of the house were standing up for Olya.

"Good-bye, Olya, come back soon."

* * * * *

Olya was a sturdy girl, well-built, red-cheeked, with a light auburn plait and thick dark brows which looked as if they had been blacked. On her first day at school she was surrounded, her cheeks were pinched, she was squeezed and pulled in all directions, but she was interested most in the clothes-pegs—there were so many of them in the cloakroom and it was such fun to drag your hand along them from end to end.

Praskovya Ivanovna Penkin, the head of the *pension* where Olya was put as a boarder, on the contrary, took a dislike to Olya from the first day.

She was thin, with close-cropped hair, green and old, and she kept making fun of Olya.

Olya prepared her lessons quickly and caused no fuss or bother, but each time she entered the classroom where the other girls were at their studies the head sent her away:

"Get out, you cow!"

Or, calling Olya up, she would begin asking what Olya cleaned her teeth with, and when Olya said she didn't clean them with anything, she dismissed her again:

"Get out, you cow!"

Olya was very offended when she was called such names, and she didn't like Praskovya Ivanovna.

Olya felt insults very deeply.

Once, in Vatagino, Olya and her elder sister Irena went for a walk in the woods with the steward. At one point they had to cross a stile. Irena clambered over quickly, but Olya—then quite small—scrambled and scrambled, and couldn't do it.

"Such a small bubble and it tries to go too!" the steward laughed, and picking her up he carried her over.

Olya was very offended: she cried a whole week, but she wouldn't say for anything why she was crying.

Later, Olya showed she was offended differently—not by silent tears.

But even now there were no silent tears; Olya just tried to avoid Praskovya Ivanovna. There were a lot of absorbing things in the *pension* and somehow the insult was forgotten.

On Saturdays, about ten, when the girls had gone to bed, Praskovya Ivanovna Penkin used to have visitors.

The guests were all their own people, mostly masters, women teachers and the form mistresses from the Pokidosh Girls' School. They all disposed themselves round the big drawing-room, one of the doors of which opened on to the room where the girls of the lowest form slept.

Olya's bed stood just by this door, and usually on Saturdays Olya didn't fall asleep until the guests separated, and it always seemed to her that there were so many of them that there'd be no room for an apple to drop.

Amongst the guests there was their favourite Yakov Stepanovich Theophilactov, the physics and geography master, with his one lip and cleft nose, and he would tell stories in just as lively a way as in class about his travels through Russia with his knowing friend; and the most terrifying master of all, the historian Philemon Petrovich Kurapov-Taptiga, who always said when he met a lady: "My respects, dear lady!" in the style popular with dandified Pokidosh shopkeepers: "Good day, allow me! . . ."; and the menace of the school, Katerina Feodorovna, who made you solve problems from the end and added her nota-benes; and the three form mistresses, Marya Petrovna, Marya Dimitrievna, Marya Terent'evna—dry and green, somehow re-sembling both the Head of the school, Marya Ivanovna, and the Head of the *pension*, Praskovya Ivanovna, even though nothing ever came out in their conversation to suggest they were in any way related; then also Father Aristotelev, the scripture master, of whom it was said that after the discovery of sacred relics in Pokidosh he built himself a house on the proceeds of the relics, just as it was said of the dentist famous in Pokidosh that he had built himself a house on Pokidosh teeth.

Sometimes the other priest, Father Svobodin, the scripture master in the junior forms, also came. This priest was well liked in the school, and in town he was invariably called Job of the Sorrows.

In one winter his wife and his son died of galloping con-sumption, and in the spring his youngest daughter was drowned. And there was such a muddle over that accident: it was awful. In the confusion they couldn't make out who was drowned—both the priest's daughters had been out bathing—and when they started searching the river, someone ran and told the priest that the eldest, Katya, who was in Olya's form, was drowned. Then a little later Katya came home: to be sure she was rather oddly dressed, just in her shift and her hat, but he had no eyes for that, he was overjoyed, it was as if she had risen from the dead, and he thought no one was drowned, that there had been a mistake—and at this point, they dragged the youngest out and carried her home dead. Olya was at the funeral and saw how terrifying it was: the priest couldn't walk and he crawled on all fours after the coffin all the way from the house to the church, and afterwards from the church to the graveyard.

Father Svobodin was quiet, you could hardly hear him; that would be Taptiga, Philemon Petrovich the historian, it was not a voice he had but some sort of cast iron.

But the most important and sought-after guest, though he came but seldom, was the literature master, Paul Nikolaivich Solov'ev. If Yakov Stepanovich was liked and Philemon Petrovich was feared, Paul Nikolaivich was adored, and not only by the eldest girls whom he taught literature but by the youngest, too, from hearsay.

You could have made three Paul Nikolaiviches out of one Yakov Stepanovich, and he was polite, he didn't even look like a teacher, he never addressed the girls other than as "Miss So-and-so," he had gold-rimmed spectacles, a small nose with a scratch on it, a moustache and a little tufted beard, he never caught you out, never reported you, and he expressed his highest displeasure with the remark:

"You write compositions like cooks."

And if Philemon Petrovich had got hold of any of the compositions which merely called forth this remark from Paul Nikolaivich, what wouldn't Philemon Petrovich have done in his place?

Here is an essay by Nadya Vorob'ev in the VIIth form on "What are the signs of friendship between comrades?"

"On separation friends usually die or go mad. This happens with young friends who are also of different sexes. This is called infatuation. If it does not go off for a long time, it is called love. The End."

Of course, with Philemon Petrovich that *would* be the end—an enormous bewhiskered "one" taking up four whole squares.

Paul Nikolaivich knew of no such whiskers and gave a "three" with three minuses, but wrote so faintly that sometimes he himself could take it for a "five" at the final adding up.

As soon as Paul Nikolaivich arrived at the evening gathering a twitter rose in the *pension*; they twittered round him and made up to him as if he were an idol, all the three form mistresses, the dry green ones and Praskovya Ivanovna herself. And where did

those voices come from—such melting, melting tones which neither the form-room nor the school ever heard even on holidays—
the usual voice in class was notorious: hoarse from the depths and
shrill—but here!

* * * * *

The evening opened with the samovar being brought in;
they drank tea and then sat down to cards, and afterwards
walked about the room in pairs or ran from corner to corner—
that's how Olya imagined it behind the door.

In fact after the second or third samovar and refreshments
they danced and played forfeits and general post. When Paul
Nikolaivich came everything was different: Paul Nikolaivich
sang romances.

Behind the door in the room where the girls slept, the singing could be heard brokenly, but the girls did not only want to
hear the singing—after all, what is singing!—they wanted to see
how Paul Nikolaivich sang: that's what they aimed at.

One Saturday the rumour went round that Paul Nikolaivich
would be present for sure. And they decided not to go to sleep,
even if it meant keeping awake the whole night, but to wait for
a suitable moment during the singing and to open the door ajar.

Olya's bed was the strategic point for observation, and when
the music was heard, Olya stood up on her bed, and leaning on
it with her arms, gently pushed it forward—the door opened
and the crack came directly opposite Paul Nikolaivich.

Paul Nikolaivich was holding the music in one hand and
adjusting his collar with the other in preparation to start.

At the moment when Paul Nikolaivich began to sing:

"'Neath the sweet-smelling bough of the lilac
She and I watched the slumbering stream . . ."

they pressed so hard on Olya from behind, pushed and squeezed
her so, that her hands on the door gave way—the door was flung
open and Olya bounced into the room.

Consternation! Praskovya Ivanovna and all three form
mistresses—Marya Petrovna, Marya Dimitrievna, and Marya
Terent'evna at first were frozen into immobility and—luckily—

Olya had fallen into the drawing-room in her nightdress—the shame
of it!

were speechless: Olya had fallen into the drawing-room in her nightdress—the shame of it!

They went for her properly.

* * * * *

Olya spent her first school year in Praskovya Ivanovna Penkin's *pension*.

The happiest days of that year and of all her school years for Olya were her father's visits: Alexander Pavlovich used to come to Pokidosh for the elections.

Usually in the early morning, before school, when they had only just got up, Olya would catch a glimpse of an approaching carriage, of her father's blue hat-band and Nicholas I coat, and she would drop everything—all her books—and run out to meet him. And she kissed him, wouldn't let him take his things off, embraced him with her small hands, still hot from sleep, and was so glad, so glad she nearly wept.

And he would give her a little hamper from home, with a chicken, poppy-seed cakes with honey, jam, fruit pastilles.

"My small kitten," he would say, "what a big daughter you're getting to be, it's not by the year you grow, but by the hour," and he would smile.

And Olya felt more happy still: she didn't know where to begin telling him things, and she wanted to look into the little hamper quickly and see what it held.

Not long before the summer holidays Natalya Ivanovna arrived from Vatagino, and on hearing of Olya's life *en pension*, she was very dissatisfied—Olya's hair had to be cut short—there was such dirt everywhere and no supervision.

* * * * *

Next year Olya was not sent to the *pension* but to some friends, the Bersenevs.

The Bersenevs were of an old Pokidosh family, and Bersenev himself had at one time held an important office but had later retired. Sonya Bersenev was in the same form as Olya, and moreover they had music lessons from the same teacher, so that Olya wanted to live with her friend.

If everything did not go quite smoothly in the Penkin *pension*—and had Praskovya Ivanovna been just a trifle more friendly Olya would probably have got used to it—at the Bersenevs, on the other hand, everything went very well, and there was only one thing—it was frightening.

Bersenev himself, Sonya's father, was a strange man, and the Bersenevs' house was not an ordinary one.

There was a story in the town that the house was haunted and that as soon as it was purchased someone in the family invariably died. Usually houses like that stand vacant and pass easily into the hands of the first buyer. The Bersenevs bought the house very cheaply.

The Bersenev family consisted of the father and his two daughters: the eldest, Nalya, was already grown up and occupied herself with housekeeping; the youngest, Sonya, was a schoolgirl; and there was a son and another daughter, but these lived in St. Petersburg.

Bersenev's strangeness came out in the fact that after his wife's death he never spoke to his children, although he spoke and even joked with other people, with Olya for instance.

Nalya and Sonya, who, incidentally, bore a strong facial resemblance to their father, had got accustomed to this and had evolved a special technique for their intercourse with him.

So when Sonya wanted to have a party, she went up to her father and asked his permission to invite some schoolfriends, and without waiting for a reply went into her room. If there were some sweets, fruit and *hors d'œuvres* waiting on the piano in the morning, that meant that her father had given his permission.

He would sit silent at tea and at dinner as if they were not only not present at the table but as if they did not even exist in this world, but in spite of this any wishes the sisters let fall in their conversation were always obligingly realised for them. Once over tea, chattering to Olya about pretty clothes, Sonya started dreaming of a warm brown jersey, which she decided to buy herself without fail as soon as she got some money—the very next morning a warm brown jersey lay on the piano.

When Nalya, the eldest, decided to get married and asked her father for his blessing he did not say a word even at the time, only snorted slightly—but in the morning two ikons, some candles and some money were lying on the piano.

Olya gazed with wide eyes at the father's strange intercourse with his children, but later grew used to that and stopped paying attention, only she could not fail to notice the things that went on about the house.

Not all but some of the parquet blocks and somehow in circular groups used to creak in a special way even during the day-time, and this creaking seemed to drag at your heart.

And if they forgot to close the piano for the night someone played softly on it, only so softly!—this soft playing made you feel gloomy and you wouldn't find a place for yourself away from this gloom where you could sleep.

Before lying down Olya and Sonya would make the sign of the cross over each other and cover all the mirrors; there was something unpleasant in the mirrors, a kind of ghostly light, and of course that was frightening.

Olya only had to live for a few months in this good but singular family's haunted house. Both the son and daughter who lived in St. Petersburg suddenly died, and the Bersenevs' house was immediately sold for a mere song.

Natalya Ivanovna moved to Pokidosh with little Lena, took a flat, and for a month Olya lived with her mother.

But very soon Natalya Ivanovna was compelled to return to Vatagino, and Olya went to live *en pension* with two German ladies—Paulina Vikent'evna and Rosalia Vikent'evna Linde.

III

The *pension* Linde was an exemplary one and Paulina Vikent'evna and Rosalia Vikent'evna were ladies of good family.

Paulina Vikent'evna was married and Rosalia Vikent'evna was unmarried. They were alike, both were tiny and round-shouldered, with exceptionally long noses and exceptionally small

childish lips, both were covered in wavy wrinkles, fine and delicate as a cobweb, and on the head of each there rested a black
lace cap. And the only difference between them was that Paulina
Vikent'evna had some right, even if a remote one, to wear a
married woman's dress, whilst if Rosalia Vikent'evna affected it,
and had, they said, done so now for forty years, it was only
through a pure misconception.

Paulina Vikent'evna had three sons who were all exceptionally tall—nearly touched the ceiling: the two eldest, a doctor and
a student, lived in St. Petersburg, and only came on visits to
their mother in Pokidosh, the youngest served in the provincial
court of chancery and lived with his mother at the *pension*.

The girls liked the doctor and the student: in cases of mis-
understanding the doctor and the student always took their side.
But they did not like the youngest, the clerk in chancery, and
called him a spy: he informed his mother and aunt whenever,
for instance, a schoolgirl was seen home from a visit by a schoolboy, and even though the girls found a way out by saying it was
not a schoolboy at all, but a footman with silver buttons, still
unpleasantness did sometimes result.

Paulina Vikent'evna said not once or twice but many a time:

"I was pretty, but Rosalia Vikent'evna was simply beautiful."

"No, I was pretty, but Paulina Vikent'evna was simply
beautiful!" Rosalia Vikent'evna would invariably reply.

Paulina Vikent'evna would not agree for anything, an argument would ensue and the whole *pension* would nearly die
laughing.

Paulina Vikent'evna and Rosalia Vikent'evna would wax
more talkative after dinner than at any other time, and then
they shared their reminiscences willingly.

"Once Rosalia Vikent'evna and I went to a ball," Paulina
Vikent'evna related, "and as we arrived late our beaux wanted
to pay us out for this, and no one asked us to dance; so then we
just started to dance together. This was so sweet that all the
gentlemen left their ladies and came to dance with us."

"Ach, it was so sweet, so sweet, goodness me, it was so sweet!" the two German ladies repeated in chorus.

Someone started the rumour that Paulina Vikent'evna and Rosalia Vikent'evna went about in rubber skirts.

There were many conversations about this, but the greatest puzzle was: what were these rubber skirts like—were they like galoshes or like a ball?

Everyone wanted to see these rubber skirts, but how could you have a look when the two German ladies never made an appearance before the girls, let alone in rubber skirts, but never even without their black lace caps—Germans are meticulous in their personal appearance, Germans like order.

But once the girls started a great commotion as they were getting into bed, and Paulina Vikent'evna and Rosalia Vikent'evna, not knowing what to think and forgetting all about order, rushed into the room in a state of undress, and?—each one—this everyone noticed without even looking—had on a real rubber skirt.

"Look, but they danced in these skirts!" Olya shouted gleefully.

"Ach, it was so sweet, so sweet, goodness me, it was so sweet!" they heard the German ladies saying, and they hardly slept a wink, choking with laughter all night.

About three times a year the Pastor came to Pokidosh, and then Paulina Vikent'evna and Rosalia Vikent'evna disappeared from the *pension*.

Someone said that when the Pastor took the service the two German ladies sang.

And this seemed far more comical than the rubber skirts: it was as hopelessly funny and impossible as it would be if Father Aristotelev dressed up as an officer.

The German ladies were tiny, thin, round-shouldered and all nose, certainly no songstresses, and the clergyman with his little paunch, old boots for lips, a shoe nose and a habit of drawing his lips together when he talked so that not a single tooth could be seen—a fine officer!

They laughed at school in the middle of lessons, they laughed in the *pension* over their homework and on walks and in church, just suddenly for nothing at all, at the mere thought of the German ladies singing and of the clergyman as an officer.

They had a good deal of freedom. You could go for a walk out in the street without anyone and at any time.

One of the girls would run out and ring the bell, and another would tell Paulina Vikent'evna or Rosalia Vikent'evna that a maid had been sent for her, and permission was given. In this way the girls managed to get out even when they were not due for lessons at the school, and such walks were seventh heaven to them.

It was free and easy and they were all happy with the two Germans. The only thing was they weren't given overmuch to eat, and the girls often took black bread from the sideboard, and at tea-time put away plain white French bread with great appetite, their whole jaws creaking. But you couldn't do anything about that: a *pension* is not like home.

"Squash the bread before you eat it and pretend it's got cheese in it, and when you've had enough, pretend there's *khalva** in it," Princess Shakh-Bulatov, who was in the VIth, taught the hungry Olya.

Olya did as she had said: she squashed the bread as close as she could before she ate it, and did her best to pretend it contained cheese, and when she finished she tried to pretend it had *khalva* in it.

And the lesson was a profitable one.

The two German ladies treated Olya very well, but for some reason they took it into their heads that Olya's eyebrows were not natural and kept reprimanding her for painting them. And even though Olya would lick her finger and draw it across her eyebrows and her finger would remain absolutely clean, the Germans would not believe her.

*   *   *   *   *

---

* A sweetmeat of honey and nuts.   *Translator's Note.*

Olya was attracted by people older than herself, and she was always hanging about the room where the older girls did their lessons.

Olya had taken a great liking to two VIth form girls when she was still in the Ist form. They were Vera Sakharova and Princess Shakh-Bulatov.

Vera Sakharova was tall and strong but very pale, just like white marble with enormous black eyes and black hair brushed smoothly back—Olya though her beautiful.

Princess Shakh-Bulatov was rosy, dark-browed with golden curls, large blue eyes and exceptionally long eyelashes, and she was very slim—Olya called her a Beauty.

In her first days at school when Olya met the princess she smiled at her, blew her kisses and once she asked her name, but the princess made no reply, and Vera Sakharova answered for her that the princess's name was Marya Alexandrovna.

"Marya Alexandrovna, Princess Shakh-Bulatov," Olya repeated afterwards, and she drew the letters on a damp glass:

M A P S

Once, returning from vespers to the *pension*, Olya met a roving pilgrim. The pilgrim stopped Olya and gave her a little white pebble, "Our Lady's tear," and the prayer, "Our Lady's dream."

"If you write your wish on to the end of the prayer," the pilgrim had said, "and always wear the prayer on you, your wish will come true."

In the *pension* that evening—that was when she was still at Praskovya Ivanovna's—Olya copied out the prayer through a blue transfer paper, and she did it like that because in her opinion the blue colour had some very special significance. To this blue prayer, this "Our Lady's dream," she added her wish in blue:

"Lord, make me like Princess Shakh-Bulatov!"

And while she was copying out the prayer she conjured up a picture in her mind of Vera Sakharova, who was beautiful, and of Princess Shakh-Bulatov, who was a Beauty, and at the same time she thought somehow of her first teacher, Sophia Evdokimovna, Vatagino's Father Evdokim's daughter, who was the cleverest. Then she sewed the prayer into her amulet,* put it round her neck and waited to see what would happen.

A long week passed. On Saturday Olya asked one of the girls whether she saw any difference in her.

"No," the girl answered, "I can't see any."

"Not in any way?"

"You're just the same."

"Vera Sakharova is beautiful," thought Olya, "and Princess Shakh-Bulatov is a Beauty, well let one be beautiful and the other a Beauty!" and she took off her amulet.

Vera Sakharova and Princess Shakh-Bulatov were the most hopeless, the most frivolous and the most often rebuked of all the girls in the *pension*. They always had visits from young men on Sundays. And although it was well known that the princess was from Moscow where her mother and father lived and that she had no relations in Pokidosh except an old grandmother, still all kinds of brothers kept turning up and hanging about the waiting-room all day, until the German ladies smoked them out and then only with the aid of the "March of the Russian Volunteers." There was a piano in the waiting-room and one of the youngest girls was sent to play this "March of the Russian Volunteers" until the young men went off home of their own accord.

"Listen," Paulina Vikent'evna once said to Princess Shakh-Bulatov when it was obvious that her suspicions had overcome her kindheartedness, trustfulness and delicacy: "Why is your brother sometimes fair, sometimes dark and sometimes chestnut-haired "

"That's very simple," the Princess retorted: "in the morning he's chestnut, at midday he's fair and in the evening he's dark."

But it did not always end so simply. There were occasions which could not have been got round without the aid of Paulina Vikent'evna's sons, the doctor and the student. Only the doctor

---

* A little bag containing sacred things worn by the orthodox with their baptismal crosses.   *Translator's Note.*

and the student, though they were very nice, were sometimes as clumsy as bears.

Either from information her son, the clerk in chancery, gave her or from her own observation, more likely the former, Paulina Vikent'evna, after the "March of the Russian Volunteers,"called Vera Sakharova up and gave her a strong reprimand, forbidding her in future to receive the brother-schoolboy who had just gone, as he was no brother of hers.

Vera Sakharova started arguing mulishly and Paulina Vikent'evna was beside herself, she got so angry. There was an uproar and Vera Sakharova had to give in and admit it.

The doctor came hurrying in at the noise and, not waiting to hear the matter through to the end, broke in:

"You must believe her," he told his mother, "I'm certain it was her brother, I saw with my own eyes how they kissed when they said good-bye."

And there was a second uproar, this time on account of the kiss.

When they went out for walks in a crocodile, Vera Sakharova and Princess Shakh-Bulatov always went together right at the very tail-end, and behind them was another crocodile of schoolboys. They were not allowed to talk to the boys during walks but Vera Sakharova always did talk. They tried to reprimand her but she took no notice. And they started leaving her behind at the *pension*, without any walk.

At this all the fury of the irresponsible marble-white schoolgirl burst out: she ran about the room as though she were possessed and flung whatever came to hand without aiming at anyone, banged the doors and swore at the two Germans by everything she could think of.

As the Germans did not understand everything in Russian, some of the expressions were not exactly vulgar but still unprintable, and the further it went, the stronger and more abusive the language.

If all that abuse had lighted on the poor Germans nothing would have remained of them—just a flat pancake.

The giddy Vera Sakharova loved to laugh at the younger girls and to tease them: she'd snatch a book from under the very nose of one of them or hide it in secret, and the girl would go about with nothing to learn her lesson from, begging for the book, but no, she'd not give it back for anything, until next morning when it was time to go to class and then she'd slip it across.

Both Vera Sakharova and Princess Shakh-Bulatov liked Olya very much and never drove her from their room. Olya used the second person plural to them and they addressed Olya in the second person singular, or sometimes called her "you owl" because of her large grey eyes.

Everyone in the *pension* knew that Olya was very talented and one of the best pupils. Knowing Olya's good nature Vera Sakharova and Princess Shakh-Bulatov examined her in Russian grammar, when they asked her questions to which the right answers willy-nilly fell into the class of unprintable words used by Vera Sakharova herself in her rages.

And Olya smiled, gazing at the marble-white fury who was "beautiful" and at the passionate golden princess who was a "Beauty," and she felt happy.

IV

Among the girls of her own age Olya made friends with Marina Zavetnovsky, who was in her own form.

To look at, Marina was the very opposite of Olya: she was small, pale and thin, but she was as alert as Olya. They ran about the hall together during break, together they arranged all kinds of rags at the school and in the *pension*, and once during dancing they were standing *vis-à-vis* and they kissed—a kiss that got the whole class punished. The handiwork mistress, who was also their form mistress and was nicknamed the Heron, and who did not like either Olya or Marina, called them quite simply: "The two specimens."

And as though on purpose the Heron, who kept a watch on the girls in the street, often chanced to meet Olya and Marina when they slipped out on the quiet from the *pension* for a walk.

"Where are you going?" the Heron would ask.

"For my exercise book."

"It should be written across your face that you are going for your book," the Heron would lecture, "you should walk with a quick, sharp step."

Olya was particularly friends with Marina Zavetnovsky, though she was friends with everyone in her class, even though her Aunt, Marya Petrovna, made distinctions about girls with whom Olya should not be friends as they were not her equals.

"It doesn't matter so much now," Olya heard her Aunt tell Natalya Ivanovna both at Vatagino and Pokidosh, "but when they grow up, it will not be decent for Olya to go to some houses, to the Rogachevs for instance—Mme Rogachev is living with the public prosecutor—or to the Saburovs—they keep a guest-house!"

And Olya was not allowed to visit some of the girls. But it was just to these that Olya would go; she asked the Germans for leave to visit the ones she was allowed to visit and then went to the others.

Marina Zavetnovsky was amongst those forbidden by Aunt, as her father was an actor in a travelling company now playing for the second year in the Pokidosh municipal theatre.

* * * * *

The town of Pokidosh, sung by a local poet whose modest wish it was to remain anonymous, is in some ways the first-mother of all Russian towns—the cradle of Russia.

"Pokidosh is an ancient town
    Built on the river Smurga, moreover
    Its harbour is of excellent renown . . ."

In Pokidosh, where an important personage of the town at the unveiling of a statue to a famous Russian author, once announced in his peroration to the inhabitants of Pokidosh that the statue cost so and so much good money and must therefore be taken as much care of as a shrine, while in the square the police-man drove off all those who stood gaping at the statue with a "Pass on there, there's nothing to see!"—where an eccentric governor had a marble obelisk erected to himself in the cathedral square with a list of all his services to the province and a notice was displayed on a post nearby: "Sunflower-seed husks and fruit peel must not be dropped here. By Order"—where the Chief Constable issued an order to the populace on the eve of a lunar eclipse that they were not to gape at the sky for nothing if it turned out cloudy; where they always apologised in the kindness of their hearts when they offered their clergyman pie with egg filling (it had no double meaning if you took things straight-forwardly); where from time immemorial a mysterious brigand of one sort or another had always been at large and was always the equal in daring of Savitzky and Lbov if not of Solovey* himself; where people built houses with the aid of sacred relics, teeth and objects of even greater delicacy; where for a long while back now the old watchman no longer kept a look-out on the watch-tower for fires but it only seemed to everyone from habit that he was still there; where they still tolled the alarm-bell for fires and all the inhabitants turned out as they did for church at Easter; where the young ladies almost without exception discovered that they had a talent for acting and suddenly wanted to become actresses; where at evening parties if an eccentric brought up any deep and weighty, though perhaps untimely, problem, he was greeted with a burst of healthy Russian monkey laughter; and where, finally, in the public park in spring, drunk with dew from the young birch leaves, the nightingale sang till the whole garden shook—everything was there—in every key: gurgles, trills, tre-molos, crescendos, quivers, the pipes of Pan, the cuckoo's cry, wild geese, the lark's shrilling, ebbing and flowing, every kind of whistle, trill and noise—in this quiet, peaceful and dusty Poki-dosh, Marya Petrovna Vol'sky played no minor part.

---

* The robber-hero of Russian folklore.

Marya Petrovna Vol'sky's husband, Olya's uncle, was a retired captain who was in receipt of an enormous pension for wounds: one of Uncle's eyes was not his own but an artificial china eye. Uncle had lost his eye in the Turkish campaign: he was returning home once from a Pokidosh holiday which had been arranged in town on the occasion of receiving some important war news, when he fell from the horse-cab and injured his eye so seriously that it was as bad as if a bullet had lodged in it.

Marya Petrovna herself, who in her turn was agitating for the pension, assured everyone that it was not a bullet at all but seventy-seven Turkish explosive shells.

And copying Marya Petrovna, the whole of Pokidosh, when repeating this unfortunate story of Uncle and the cab on suitable and unsuitable occasions, always added:

"And seventy-seven Turkish explosive shells."

Uncle liked telling about engagements by sea and land, and often recalled campaigns, battles and the storming of fortresses. And Olya and her cousin Lenochka, Uncle's daughter, listened to these wonderful stories with tremendous attention.

Marya Petrovna was a model mother and an exemplary bringer-up of children.

When she was only five Lenochka could answer without any hesitation even when she had just woken out of her sleep the three basic family questions:

"Who is your Mamma?"

"Know-all."

"Who is your Pappa?"

"Do-all."

"And you?"

"Lenochka."

These responses enraptured the whole of Pokidosh and all this was the absolute truth.

Marya Petrovna really did know everything; she appeared absolutely everywhere, at all the *soirées*, the funerals, the weddings—no one made merry, or buried their dead or married without her, they even somehow managed to fall ill under her eye, she had a finger in everything, liked to know of everything and she talked about everything, she could speak of everything and not only relate all the ins and outs of the past but sometimes even of the future—things which were only anticipated and were far from realised. And Uncle, with his china eye, really could mend Lenochka's broken dolls amazingly deftly and carefully even on the occasions when the dolls' makers would not agree to undertake the job for any sum and refused point-blank.

Since she talked a great deal herself, Marya Petrovna valued above everything what people said. The final indisputable argument overcoming every doubt was for her this: "they say."

"Olya, what is this people are saying about you?" Aunt would demand, smoking her cigarette, and she immediately passed on one of the Pokidosh rumours which left even Aunt's own assurances about the seventy-seven Turkish explosive shells in Uncle, far behind.

When Natalya Ivanovna came from Vatagino and stopped with the Vol'skys, amid the hail of Pokidosh news Aunt's "they say" would stick in the conversation like a wedge.

"Just imagine, Natalya Ivanovna, Zina Raev goes to the public park and she's going to have a baby soon."

"But that's impossible."

"Natalya Ivanovna, *they say* so!"

She would take a breath, draw herself up and begin again:

"Just imagine: Liza Shalaurov sent Olya Bogdanovich a soldier with a letter and they say Shalaurov himself sent it."

"No, Marya Ivanovna, surely?"

"Natalya Ivanovna, *they say* so!"

"Aunt keeps saying things which aren't true," Olya thought on the rare occasions when the conversation reached her ears.

"Why do you say such silly untrue things?" Olya thumped the table angrily, but that was much later when she was already in the VIIth form, now she just thought about it and noticed it.

Drinking tea with cream was Marya Petrovna's favourite occupation when there was nothing to say or no one to talk to.

Olya and Lenochka were given milk in their tea, but she added cream to her own and the thicker and richer the cream the kinder and softer grew her heart and the more benevolent her mood, whilst she herself was all sharp like a needle, with little black eyes like whirligigs, and it was impossible to say where the thick rich food, this sweet cream, disappeared.

Anna Pavlovna, their favourite Granny's ambassadress, usually put up at Marya Petrovna's.

Trying to make use of the old Mezheninka housekeeper's good mood, Olya and, following her example, Lenochka too, begged her to tell them something about the past.

To which Anna Pavlovna agreed.

"When I was young I was a great beauty," Anna Pavlovna used to say. "I had enormous blue eyes, long hair—it used to get caught in my shoes, I had long eyelashes, they stood right out from my face, and I had a suitor, Peter Ivanovich. He stood by my chair once," Anna Pavlovna dropped her gaze down languidly "and he said, 'Anna Pavlovna!' I said, 'What?' And he said, 'Have you seen a great fire?' and I said, 'Yes.' And he said, 'In a fire every flame burns, burns and dies, but my love for you, Anna Pavlovna, shall never die.' He said this to me and I sat there knitting my eyelashes into little knots."

Olya told this story about the eyelashes to Marina Zavetnovsky in the *pension*. Marina had very short eyelashes and she wanted to have eyelashes exactly like Anna Pavlovna's so that she could knit them into little knots.

"I expect they sell some sort of ointment for it," Olya said. "You put it on and your eyelashes grow long as long."

Where could you get this ointment and what was it: whitening?—no; politan? You only put politan on cats. They thought a lot about it and they thought for a long time but they couldn't think of anything. They asked Vera Sakharova for advice.

"You *can* get it," Vera Sakharova said, and promised she would.

About three days later a little tin with some sort of sticky filth passed like a treasure into the hands of Olya and Marina.

That same day, without any procrastination, Olya carefully painted Marina's eyelashes for the night. Her tears fell like hail and the thin pale little girl sneezed and sneezed—goodness alone knows how she slept through that night. And next morning when she started washing the ointment off, everything came with it and she lost all the eyelashes she ever had.

V

Olya was a great tomboy, everyone at the high school knew of the pranks she got up to, everyone in the IVth form, all the girls in the *pension* with the two German ladies. But an observant eye would discern that Olya lived another life about which she would never say a word to other people.

This hidden life of hers began before she went to school when she was still in the country at Vatagino.

It often happened that Olya would stand stock-still in one place motionless and would go on standing like that for hours. Just try and guess why she stood stock-still, thinking, on her guard, and when she was called she didn't reply at once? Honestly, the answer to the riddle would never occur to you.

Can you imagine the reason? No! Olya was waiting for the Last Judgement.

Olya dreamt of the Last Judgement twice.

The first time she dreamt there were a great many people among the raspberry bushes and they all stood there side by side while the clergyman read to them—this was the Last Judgement.

Another time she dreamt that someone said to her:

"The Last Judgement will be tomorrow."

This last dream made a tremendous impression on Olya who was seven years old then—now she was twelve—and she worried about it as much as any grown-up would have done.

She woke up and didn't close her eyes again: one problem alone tormented her and she couldn't solve it—how was she to understand that "tomorrow?" She asked herself: "Will the Last

Judgement take place this morning, or only next day, to-morrow?"

And she couldn't decide.

The whole morning and the whole day she passed in expectation. And here an incident took place, quite an innocent one in itself, but Olya who was worked up even without it now grew more worried still.

Two little neighbours, Leda and Anya Sakhnovsky, came to Vatagino. To amuse her friends Olya showed them her exercise books: these exercise books had words and letters printed in them in fine strokes. Olya herself still wrote pretty badly and if she had traced over the print with her pen—which was what the books were really for—the result would have been most untidy. Well, you couldn't surprise anyone with scrawls and blots, so Olya gave out to the two little girls that the printed words and letters were her own, which she alleged she had just written. Leda and Anya squealed and clapped their hands in delight, and this amused Olya so much and she was so pleased that for the moment she forgot all about her dream and its prediction.

But no sooner had the Sakhnovsky girls driven away than the whole thing began again: to the thought that tomorrow it would be the Last Judgement was added her repentance at having told an untruth before such a terrible day.

She didn't know what she ought to do.

Should she ask to be allowed to go with her brother Misha to the Sakhnovskys immediately and there admit everything to Leda and Anya——

"No," Olya thought, "that's too shameful—but if I don't admit it, it's very frightening."

What was she to do?

She spent the night like the previous one, in anxiety, never closing her eyes, seized with fear and repentance. She waited till morning without going to sleep—and nothing happened. She got up, dressed, the day went by—and nothing happened.

"Apparently the Last Judgement has been postponed!" Olya decided, and felt better.

And she had quite calmed down and begun to forget her deception of the day before, when suddenly at twilight she heard a bell tinkle on the way towards their house. Olya leapt up to see who it was coming—she was a terribly curious child—and she froze where she stood. For it was no other than Leda and Anya's mother who was coming and it was obvious why.

"Of course," Olya decided, "Leda and Anya have told their mother how I tricked them with my exercise books yesterday and now she's coming to tell Mummy all about it."

And she imagined how in about an hour or no, in less, this very minute the whole house would know and everyone would call her, Olya, a fibber, a deceiver, would laugh and laugh, shame her for life and would never believe another word she said, didn't believe her now already—Olya froze where she stood.

Of course none of this happened, just as the Last Judgement never happened, but from that day the thought of the Last Judgement never left Olya.

Once on a spring morning Olya crept out into the porch before she had dressed, in her nightgown—it was warm outside, the first leaves had only just appeared and the first blades of grass, tender and small, gazed for the first time on the light—and Olya's glance fell on a duck: the duck went waddling across the yard, quacking.

"Our Lady," Olya thought, "will go like that before the Last Judgement to collect sinners!"

Olya thought a good many thoughts about how and when the Last Judgement would take place, and the thought that it might happen at any moment made her stand stock-still.

That is why sometimes Olya would stand in one place motionless, without stirring—she was waiting for the Last Judgement.

* * * * *

The thought of death became linked with the thought of the Last Judgement.

Olya used to tell her younger sister Lena that an old gnome lived in the black poplar by the woodshed and he had five children, one of his daughters was called Anya, and Olya used to visit him and he threw her apples. Lena believed her and kept asking Olya to take her to taste the gnome's apples and to have a look at the gnome himself. Olya promised to ask the gnome whether he would like that, but she kept putting it off.

Lena fell ill, she was very bad and they said she was dying. And Olya passed many a heavy unbearable day till Lena got better.

She wore herself out: she wanted to tell Lena that there wasn't any gnome in the black poplar and she saw that it was useless to say anything as Lena was past caring for gnomes now, and she tormented herself with the thought that Lena would die and she would not be able to tell her the truth about the gnome and never would be able to tell her about it now.

Olya had another sister, Tanya, who was the youngest of them all and died when she was quite tiny. On the day of Tanya's death their mother told Olya to rock Tanya. Olya didn't want to—she went out into the garden with Misha to build huts under the plum tree. And when she came in from the garden Tanya was not there any more—she was dead.

Olya passed many a heavy unbearable day: why hadn't she rocked Tanya that time? Now she would never be able to rock her again.

And when Granny died and her father told Olya that anybody might die at any moment, Olya began to fear death.

Olya expected death in the same way as she expected the Last Judgement. She often spent sleepless nights and cried about it but she never told anyone the reason for her tears.

Olya spent whole days thinking how she could prevent death and at last she decided: she would run about, even if she fell ill she would still run about—then death would not take her because people always die lying down.

She ran about like a thing possessed from morning till night, it was hard to get her to sit down to table and they spent a long time persuading her to lie down in her bed at night—she'd seem to quieten down and then she would be up again—and no one could keep up with her if they went for a walk, she'd fly along as though she was on the wing.

Then suddenly Olya felt that this would not help: however much you ran, death would still come—it wouldn't look, for it hadn't looked and seen that Tanya was quite tiny still but had taken her just the same, and though Granny had been waiting for it, still she had died after Tanya—no, death would come and it wouldn't look, everyone's turn had to come, and Olya stopped running about.

Nurse Fatevna often told Olya that she would see her Granny again when her own turn came. Olya believed that she would see her but this didn't change the matter a whit: death itself remained absolutely inevitable.

Nurse Fatevna often told Olya that the dead rose from their graves on Easter Eve. Olya believed this and every time on Easter Night it seemed to her that among the old women who sat by the church with the *paskhi*, in their long white shawls like shrouds, the dead sat too.

Someone whom nobody knows and at a time which no one can foretell, takes a person's eyes away and the eyes see no more, takes their ears and the ears hear no more, takes the tongue and the tongue talks no more, pinions the arms and the legs—and you can't do anything and you can't stop it.

In Praskovya Ivanovna Penkin's *pension* the portress was the long, withered old woman Fedosya, who was like a stake. When Fedosya talked you could see her jaw moving and she was always dressed in navy blue, her skirt was blue and her blouse was blue. Fedosya was called simply the "retired" old woman. She sat in the room with a wash-hand basin where the children's clothes hung—the room was a long way from the hall and the bedrooms at the other side of the house.

One evening the girls went off to see Fedosya and begged her to tell them a story. Fedosya agreed and began telling them stories and all the tales she told were about death: and she was merry and amusing, and most of all, someone whom you couldn't leave for anything. Fedosya told her stories and her jaw moved with every word she said.

Olya never asked her to tell stories again and she began to be frightened of Fedosya, and Fedosya sat all in navy blue, withered and bony, knitting her sock in the room at the other end of the *pension*, she knitted her sock and guarded the children's clothes.

* * * * *

Olya always said her prayers and she never missed evensong.

She went to the old monastery where they let her go alone—the monastery was quite near. Olya's chest was quite covered with little crosses and sacred pictures—she had a great variety, some of copper and some of cypress wood on different coloured ribbons and cords.

At the service Olya prayed about her lessons, about Tanya, and when her mother moved to town she prayed specially for her father so that he would not be afraid as he was alone in the house and it's frightening to live alone, particularly in the autumn when trees are full of noise and dogs howl.

Olya prayed with all her heart, she had faith and was sure her prayers would be answered.

Once when her Granny was still alive, her mother had fallen very ill indeed so that the doctor was there and their clergyman came. The arrival of the clergyman with the Holy Sacraments had a great effect on Olya. Granny took all the children from their mother's room into the ballroom and told them their mother was very ill and they must pray for her. She set all the children on their knees before the ikons—it was dark and only the sacred lamp was burning. And the children prayed—they cried out and prayed in their own words, cried out that their mother should not die. And Olya couldn't remember how long she cried—she couldn't see anything, not the ikons or her brother and sisters and she couldn't hear anything—not the clock on the mantel or the others, her brother and sisters praying—and when she rose from her knees, her mother did not die, she got better.

Olya had faith and she knew that if you pray with all your heart your prayer will be answered and even death will not touch you, you can stop even death.

*   *   *   *   *

The first book which Olya read right through was called "Cast your bread upon the waters and it will return to you after many days."

This book told the history of a girl called Emma and a boy called Dominic.

And then Olya had a dream. A light chocolate-coloured material lay on the table and Emma seemed to say that this was God. Olya got so frightened that she woke up.

Olya experienced unbearable torments when she first did the New Testament and heard of the sufferings of Our Lord. She sobbed all night not knowing how to alter something which is unalterable and she couldn't reconcile herself to the thought that it was too late now and you couldn't bring those days back.

"Perhaps," thought Olya, "I ought to go to Jerusalem and do something there "

And if she didn't do that something which would alter the unalterable—how would she go on living?

Once before she went to school Olya woke up one night in Vatagino. The room where she slept was next to the dining-room and the door was open. There was an enormous antique divan in the dining-room and suddenly it seemed to her that the whole divan was occupied, that the devil was lying there.

And when this thought came to her that it was the devil lying there she distinctly heard a voice in the dining-room:

"Yes, yes, yes," the devil seemed to say.

In the German *pension* Olya would wake up and hear something move in the stove and then make a gobbling sound rather like a turkey.

"That's the devil," Olya thought.

What terrible nights followed. Everyone fell asleep and she alone stayed awake. And once she couldn't bear it any longer, she was frightened to breathe even.

"Marina!" Olya called. "Come to me."

"What is it?" Marina answered.

"Come on."

When Marina came Olya's fears redoubled.

"Supposing," she thought suddenly, "this isn't Marina, but the devil pretending to be her?"

"Make the sign of the cross," Olya whispered.

"Now you do it too!" Marina almost shouted—her eyes were wide open.

Olya crossed herself.

And Marina sat down next to her. But suddenly doubt seized Olya again and repeating the "God shall rise again" she began making the sign of the cross over Marina.

"I'm really Marina, I haven't vanished," Marina said.

And then they were not afraid of each other any more and sat side by side on the bed in a kind of fearful expectancy. And quite clearly they heard someone going by on three feet, they heard him quite clearly going by on three legs.

Huddled together they shivered the night away.

Vera Sakharova noticed that Olya was nervous at night and sometimes she draped herself in a sheet, and came softly up to Olya's bed and stood motionless, all white like white marble with her long black hair loose.

Olya knew that this was not an apparition, that it was Vera Sakharova who was beautiful, but every time when she woke and saw her there her heart stopped beating.

In the morning Vera Sakharova assured her that she hadn't even thought of making an appearance, that she had slept soundly in bed and that horrors appeared to Olya everywhere.

Quite often worn out and weary with her terrors Olya huddled under the bed and spent the night there.

Everyone knew that Vera Sakharova kept a diary and they were all dying of curiosity to see it. Vera Sakharova hid her diary, but the place where she put it was at last discovered. They only had to wait for a chance to read it. And the chance presented itself. Vera Sakharova went away on a visit and was not to be back for a long time.

Olya was against reading it and was persuading the girls not to touch the book. Olya understood that Vera Sakharova hid her diary and she could sympathise with someone taking care of her things and treasuring them. Olya had some sacred belongings too: besides her little globe and several coloured boxes she had an absolutely ordinary pencil, but one which she treasured as her very own, belonging to her alone, and she never showed this pencil to anyone. Olya imagined how offended and bitter Vera Sakharova would feel if she discovered that her book had been tampered with.

But the girls wouldn't listen to Olya. They took the diary out, extinguished the light and perched on Olya's bed under the ikon lamp they began reading.

Olya was overcome with curiosity and however much she was against it, she went to sit under the lamp too. And at the most interesting place where, after a description of all her friends it was Olya's turn—"Olya Il'menev," Goreslavskaya began reading, "is a very pretty girl of twelve" and at this very moment the ikon lamp fell down.

Olya couldn't get over it for a long time.

The Last Judgement which can happen at any moment, death which can carry you off at any moment, the devil who is more terrible than any death or any other horror, the unalterable suffering of the Lord which must be put right come what may, punishment which always overtakes you for every wrong action, and finally God, who can put off the Last Judgement, avert death, conquer all fear of the devil, alter the unalterable, and withhold punishment, and who does all this in answer to prayer, if you pray like that time when mother was dying, so that you don't hear anything, neither the clock on the mantel, nor the others, brother and sisters praying, so that you don't see anything, neither the ikons nor brother nor sisters and only cry out, pray *in your own words*—that was the secret and hidden world in which Olya lived and about which she wouldn't say a word.

Thoughts about this mysterious world receded and became obscure, but were never lost sight of altogether, and all her laughter, her pranks and jokes, could not touch these thoughts, which at any moment might float to the surface and make her head dizzy, her heart ache and her eyes weep.

Olya would be thoughtful and uncommunicative for whole weeks and then suddenly become merry, would rush about, laugh, shout, reach the very extremes of pranks and tricks, but her merriment would give place to thoughtfulness just as abruptly and Olya's ringing voice and expressive laugh would no longer be heard: silent, burrowing in her thoughts and tormenting herself she would wander about like a solitary unsociable little beast or sit in one place like an owl, staring in front of her with her large grey eyes, hearing and seeing nothing of what was going on around.

VI

There was a huge orchard which belonged to the *pension* Linde. Part of it was let out and in the other part the girls did their lessons.

It was so lovely in the gardens in autumn when on a clear quiet day all the trees seemed to catch on fire, and it was so lovely to steal apples—the very ripest and tastiest hung there, firm and rosy and their guards were eagle-eyed.

There was hardly a girl to be found who did not steal apples, even though each had brought a large store from home.

Princess Shakh-Bulatov was called away to the reception-room. Presently she came back to the garden, only not alone but with a terrible dark old lady.

"A witch," Olya said.

"A real witch," Marina agreed.

"With a hook nose," Olya said, examining the old lady.

"All black," Marina opened her eyes wide.

"Do you know why she's come, Marina?"

"She's a grandmother."

"Whose grandmother?"

"Shakh-Bulatova's."

And the old lady sat awhile talking about something with the princess and then went away.

"My Granny liked you very much, she says you have a poetic face," the princess came up to Olya when she had seen the old lady off.

Olya only gazed at her golden beauty and smiled.

In a week's time the dark old lady appeared in the garden again. It was a clear quiet day again and everything seemed to be burning and golden like the golden princess.

And the old lady sat whispering about something with the princess again as before. Then the princess rose and went up to Olya.

"Granny wants to meet you," she said.

Olya followed her.

The old lady smiled a toothless smile and showed Olya two enormous black eye-teeth.

"Granny, Olya knows the whole of *Evgenii Onegin** by heart."

"Well, recite me some *Onegin*," the old lady stroked Olya's hair, "recite me some, I like *Onegin*."

Olya began to recite. The old lady sat and listened. Olya recited for a long time.

"Will you come and see me?" the old lady interrupted.

"Yes, I'll certainly come," Olya blushed and gazed clearly into her sharp, troubled eyes.

"All right, don't forget then!" and the old lady kissed Olya. It seemed to Olya that it was not lips she had but a slippery bone, and she felt a distaste so that she turned aside afterwards and spat.

"Honestly, she's a witch, honestly!" Marina said, and her eyes were enormous.

On the following Sunday the princess and Olya set out after the morning service to see her granny.

---

* Pushkin's famous poem.   *Translator's Note.*

They returned to the *pension* for lunch.

Olya came back quite unlike herself. That evening and the following day and evening and the day after that and all three nights it was clear that something was upsetting her, only she didn't say a word to anyone and was very quiet. On the third morning when it was time to go to school, she didn't open her little caskets or look at her globe or her boxes and pencil, but just pulled her bodice tighter and left the *pension* very early, much earlier than usual.

Just at this time Natalya Ivanovna arrived quite unexpectedly from Vatagino—Olya bumped into her mother at the gate.

Amid all sorts of questions about this and that Olya told about the old lady. She explained how she had first been introduced, how she went to see her with the princess on Sunday, how they walked a long way—the granny lived beyond the clocktower on the outskirts of the town—how she had a house in a garden behind a lot of trees so that you couldn't see it at once, how clean and pleasant it was in this granny's rooms, what ikons and ikon-lamps she had, how glad the old lady was to see Olya and how she offered her chocolate and how afterwards the princess went off somewhere and Olya was left alone with the old lady.

"Olya," the granny said, when they were alone, "you must dedicate yourself to God."

"Yes," Olya replied firmly.

"You must cut off your left breast and put it under the ikons," the old lady said.

Olya was suddenly afraid and she made no reply.

"All right?"

Olya said nothing.

"You must cut off your left breast and put it under the ikons, all right?" the old lady repeated.

"All right."

"Very well, think about it and come again," the old lady kissed Olya.

Father Vasilii would go out into the fields with holy water to sprinkle the earth.

Olya related all this quite simply as something which was no longer a secret and which could now be told, and she didn't notice that her mother got up from her chair and her whole expression changed.

"Mummy, I'm ready, I shall dedicate myself to God."

And a year later, in the spring, Olya was nearly drowned—they only just managed to bring her round.

They were boating on the Sugra in the evening—there were a lot of girls and they put in to the shore and decided to bathe. They had a good bathe with a lot of fun and when they were already going ashore Zhenia Goreslavsky swam off again, got right out of her depth and began to drown. Marina dived in after her, pulled Zhenia out of the deep place and got stuck herself. Olya dived in, seized Marina by the hand and Marina pulled Olya under, pushed against her with her feet and swam out—there was no sign of Olya. The fishermen saved her. They only just managed to bring her to.

And from that time Olya's eyes seemed to grow clearer and they became as grey as the waters of a lake, sometimes tinged with green, sometimes with blue, and dark grey in an unlucky year.

CHAPTER SIX

I

At the beginning of summer as soon as the exams were over Olya used to go and stay in Mezheninka with her favourite Granny, Tatiana Alexeyevna. Mezheninka was seven versts from their Il'menev Vatagino.

St. George's Day was fine in Vatagino but it was better still in Mezheninka: Father Vasilii would go out into the fields with holy water to sprinkle the earth, and in each cottage the table would be laid with the bread-and-salt of welcome, they would pass in procession behind the cross round all the boundaries, the land would grow light, Father Vasilii would bless the corn, and all night till the third cockcrow they would sing and dance in choruses and caressing songs would flow on till after the red dawn.

*The week before Whitsun passed all in garlands of flowers and young birch-leaves—the seventh Thursday after Easter would be green, and Whitsun so hot that the red poppies blossomed in the fields. St. John's Night was good, and harvest-time burning hot, the holiday at the end of harvest was good too and the frogs sang far better than in Vatagino.

When the flush of evening faded after the bright sunset and the cuckoo's bitter call was over, when a murmuring stillness descended and even the blackbird was hushed, and the evening nightingale ceased to sing and the early one perched sleeping, not yet awake, the night alone whispered and in its starry murmur along the old pond, overgrown with willow, large circles one upon another would appear and the frogs begin to sing.

Olya was afraid of frogs but she was very fond of their singing and so she sat long on the balcony, her eyes on the night and the stars. Or it was that the night with all her stars mused over Olya, over her favourite star of spring, and sang to her delicately the song of the frogs.

How could Olya help liking Mezheninka?

*   *   *   *   *

It was quiet in Mezheninka and full of loving-kindness.

Granny Tatiana Alexeyevna, her sister—Aunt Evgenia Alexeyevna and the housekeeper Anna Pavlovna made up the whole household. Granny was the tallest and stoutest, she was very generous and her cap was always white with ruffles and a bow; Aunt was tall, rather miserly and her cap had no bow, and Anna Pavlovna was the smallest, and, as she always said of herself, unfortunate in all respects, and she wore a dark kerchief.

Granny and Anna Pavlovna liked to take a pinch of snuff

---

* At this festival the houses and churches were decorated with birch leaves, and young girls would tell fortunes by casting garlands on the water and watching to see if they sank or nòt.   *Translator's Note.*

and only Aunt never took it and was always mocking the two "tobacco-sniffers."

"It was better in the old days," Granny, Aunt and Anna Pavlovna would all say.

"Now they don't even believe in God," Aunt would remark.

"The man who does not believe in God shall creep as the creeping worm, sister."

"And what was I just saying then!" Aunt flashed her great dark eyes which had once been beautiful and were now so menacing. "What a thing to suggest . . ." and she would laugh to herself: Heaven knows, perhaps she thought Granny was making insinuations at her.

"And they proposed quite differently then," Granny said.

"Granny, how did they propose in your time then?" Olya asked.

"Not the way they'll propose to you children, but respectfully."

> "Ach, what a pity
> That clothes so pretty
> Are no more worn today;
> Soon the shawl
> And veil and all
> We'll in the cupboard lay . . ."

intoned Anna Pavlovna, unfortunate in all respects.

"Granny, how did Grandfather propose to you?"

"Why, Olya, I've forgotten by now," and she gazed with such kind clear eyes. "I only remember that we were telling fortunes on Twelfth Night and I saw myself in the mirror with Ivan Vasil'evich behind my chair. So I said to my sister Evgenia Alexeyevna, 'Look, sister, how this fortune-telling comes out all wrong: who do you think I saw—Ivan Vasil'evich!' But that's how it happened after all."

Then long unhurried stories would follow with all kinds of details and irrelevant additions, about who made proposals and how they did it.

Granny used to tell about it and then Aunt.

"A general proposed to me," Anna Pavlovna broke in, "and I refused him."

"Tell us about it, Anna Pavlovna!" Olya begged.

But Anna Pavlovna could not help looking prim and would not be persuaded for a long time.

"I was housekeeper at the Soloninovs," she began at last with undisguised enjoyment, "and General Ol'hovsky arrived and said: 'Anna Pavlovna, come and be my housekeeper!' And I said, 'Marry me and then I'll come.' He made no reply. And he had to go away empty-handed."

"But it was you who proposed and he refused you."

"Why no, certainly not! Why can't you understand, Olya? He proposed to me and I refused him"—and, no longer with any pleasure but with exasperation, she repeated what she had said word for word and was quite prepared to repeat it indefinitely: "I was housekeeper at the Soloninovs, General Ol'hovsky came and said, 'Anna Pavlovna' . . ." The tears came into her pitiful eyes.

"Now, now, don't be so annoying," Granny remarked to Olya. "The general proposed and Anna Pavlovna refused him."

Olya agreed, only she couldn't restrain herself from smiling. "Granny!"

But Granny looked as if she was angry.

"Ach, what a pity
That clothes so pretty
Are no more worn today;
Soon the shawl
And veil and all
We'll in the cupboard lay . . ."

"Granny, what songs did they sing in your day?"

"Let me see, which one can I tell you, Olya, I don't remember them now," and she gazed with such kind clear eyes. "Wait a bit, I've thought of one!" and she took Olya's chin so caressingly in her hand and began a song, she didn't sing it but she said it as if she were singing, the ancient one about the Volga,

the one about the young robber-boy, about Sten'ka Razin the
Ataman, and the beautiful maiden in the golden sash.

"We on the Volga are the only ones with the real songs,"
Aunt remarked.

"As for the songs here! They're enough to make a chicken
sneeze!" agreed Anna Pavlovna.

"Yes, they don't sing songs any longer, they've sung them
all by now," Granny shook her head.

"And they can't bake pies either—they're all so small . . ."
Anna Pavlovna continued in her own strain, "and you can't eat
the *mnishki* here."

(*Mnishki* are cheese cakes.)

"It was better in the old days," Granny, Aunt and Anna
Pavlovna all said.

By birth Granny was of Kostroma, and she got from Kostroma to Mezheninka through merest chance. Grandfather Ivan
Vasil'evich came into Mezheninka by inheritance, for his ances-
tor, an important Petrine grandee, had fallen into the Tsar's displeasure and was sent to Siberia, whence his descendants afterwards moved to the Volga. Ivan Vasil'evich with Granny and
his whole household, his daughter who was of marriageable age
and his son, arrived to take possession of the estate when he fell
ill and died; meanwhile Natasha married the squire of Vatagino,
Alexander Pavlovich Il'menev, and the son, Alexey found a position in the little provincial town. And so Granny never returned
to the Volga to her native Kostroma, but remained to live out
her life in Mezheninka.

* * * * *

It was quiet in Mezheninka and full of loving-kindness.

In spring they took out the winter frames in the windows,
they fasted during Lent, made festive preparations for Easter,
painted eggs, baked Easter cakes and made *paskhi*, in summer
they made jam, bottled, salted and dried, in autumn they put
the frames back in the windows, made festive preparations for
Christmas as for Easter, on Christmas Eve they waited for the

star, they ate *kut'ya** three times a year: a lenten one before Christmas, a rich and creamy one before the New Year, a meagre one before Twelfth Day; in winter they complained of the cold, in summer of the flies and the heat, and in autumn of the rain.

The days went by quietly and peacefully, day after day, without hurrying. In the evenings to sleep the sounder they grumbled gently at one another a little: Aunt grumbled at Granny, Granny at Aunt and both Granny and Aunt at Anna Pavlovna and Anna Pavlovna at her unfortunate fate.

It was nearly ten years ago that terrifying Aunt Alexandra Alexeyevna who had also lived in Mezheninka with Granny, died, about ten years ago that Granny and Aunt had shared their sister's possessions, and although Aunt Evgenia Alexeyevna had often subsequently gone over all the things, she still had moments of doubt as to whether their late sister's possessions had been fairly divided and whether perhaps Granny had not got more than her share. And she expressed these doubts of hers aloud.

Granny would hold her peace for a long time as if she heard nothing, then her patience would be exhausted and she would just wait for an opening to give vent to her anger.

Before going to bed, Aunt would pick up an eiderdown—there were mountains of eiderdowns in Mezheninka!—and it would just turn out sometimes that the eiderdown was not Aunt's but Natalya Ivanovna's, an Il'menev one: Granny would notice this from some sort of name-tapes and stitchings, and this would give her her opening.

"But that eiderdown is Natasha's!" Granny would pick her up.

And now Aunt would pretend not to hear and would beat up the eiderdown silently.

"But that eiderdown is Natasha's!" Granny repeated, and she went on repeating this over and over until Aunt lost her patience completely.

"Well, really, Natasha's, Natasha's! What do you think I

---

* *Kut'ya*—a dish of rice and raisins, rather like mincemeat, eaten after the Mass for the dead.　　　　　　　　　　　　*Translator's Note.*

can do to the eiderdown?" Aunt flashed her great dark eyes once so beautiful and now so menacing and laughed bitterly.

Then they would settle down for the night and sleep would reconcile them.

And another quiet, peaceful, unhurried Mezheninka day would dawn.

* * * * *

It was quiet in Mezheninka and full of loving-kindness.

They drank tea on the balcony and kept an eye on the shadows, so that they could sit in the shade throughout the day, and when the cool of the evening came and shaded Granny's wide porch, they would all three settle down in the porch, where they would linger until one of them would describe yet once again some memorable event, always with details and irrelevant additions, they would discuss this event which had so often been discussed before, sit silent a while and go in to supper.

The flowers were good in Vatagino, but in Mezheninka they were more beautiful still.

There was a flower garden round the house like the garden of Eden—with "Little-coal-in-the-fire," red with a black centre, blue and red "Dishevelled ladies," and asters and dahlias, petunias, purslane, mignonette, peonies, pansies, hollyhocks and roses. And in the garden by the pond there were a great many white and crimson rose bushes. And there were wonderful hazel bushes—nowhere else could you find nuts as good as these. And some white apples with a faint suggestion of sourness ripened there too and were delicious—this apple-tree was to be found only in Granny's garden.

How good it was to drink tea under the shade of the old limes!

The samovar would be brought and then Granny would get up and walk back to the house along the path in a leisurely way (she always carried the keys on her); there she would open a tall fragrant cupboard, take out all kinds of sweetmeats and dainties and in the same leisurely way she would return with a great heaped dish in her hands, along the same path back to the samovar under the old limes, and what good things that dish held: apples, pears, cherries and plums, all kinds of sweets, nuts and pastilles and everything you could think of for you to taste— you ate your fill and were still tempted.

How good it was to stroll with Granny in the evening out to the graveyard to the old sad crosses in the little cemetery! And what tea-trays were served at Christmas and Easter and on birthdays and saintsdays—you couldn't lift them by yourself, and among the good things were all the ones Olya liked best, for Granny's favourite granddaughter had a sweet tooth. And what books in wonderful bindings Olya discovered in the storehouse— they had been put in the storehouse ages ago and had remained there ever since—and all these books Olya was to take with her.

* * * * *

Granny's birthday was on Astius of Dyrrachium's Day.

On the day of this Mezheninka ceremony, from the time when Olya first learnt to embroider little cockerels and fir-trees in cross-stitch (she had succeeded with her first cockerel when she was twelve), she gave her Granny an embroidered blouse. And this summer Olya gave her Granny her fourth blouse and moved her Granny to tears with her gift.

"Thank you, Olyushka, thank you!" Granny repeated, and she gazed at her bright favourite with such kind clear eyes.

They all celebrated Granny's birthday. They all came to bring Granny their greetings, Natalya Ivanovna, Alexander Pavlovich, Irena, Lena and Misha.

They celebrated the birthday "left-overs" next day as well and then the visitors set off again.

And Olya would not have minded going with her people but Granny would be lonely without her. And Granny wouldn't let her go for about another week till the first white apples were ripe.

She kissed Granny countless times very hard, and Aunt a little less, and Anna Pavlovna a few times—Anna Pavlovna was rather cold!—and said goodbye to her beloved Mezheninka.

II

Two old men of the Il'menev household were famous in Vatagino: Fedot the Straight—the valet, and Fedot the Bent—the butler.

Fedot the Straight was well known because ever since he was a young man he had represented on Easter Night in the Vatagino church none other than the unclean Devil himself, a part which had later been taken over by the coachman Gregory. Fedot used to stay alone in the church when all the people came out and held the door fast in his rôle of the unclean spirit, obstinately refusing to let the procession of the cross return into the church. And it was only when the words "God shall rise again" reached him from the threshold that he was overpowered and flung the portal open to the chant "Christ is risen!" and then he ran, ran across the whole empty church to vanish somewhere down to the bottomless pit, and he played his part so cunningly and deftly, made such grimaces and contortions and looked so like the devil himself, that once the other Fedot, Fedot the Bent, chasing him as he took to his heels, couldn't restrain himself in his enthusiasm from striking him across the back and so hard that the poor wretch didn't come to till the third day after and then only just. Besides this responsible rôle at the Easter celebrations which, as you see, was a pretty risky one, he was famous too as Nurse Fatevna's husband, which seemed absolutely incredible, and although he had died five years ago now come St. Elijah's Day, people still kept saying that it had happened quite recently, well, the year before last, say.

The other Fedot, Fedot the Bent, was still alive and continued to live in the best of health and had no intention of dying; although some ninety years and more had fallen to his lot. His fame dated back to the emancipation of the serfs when he refused to accept his freedom and remained in the Il'menevs' house to continue serving the family faithfully and leally as a serf. All the storehouse keys had been in his care for decades and accidents never happened to anything.

Whenever their oldest aunt, Lyudmila Pavlovna, arrived in Vatagino (she was Alexander Pavlovich's sister) she was always as glad to see the old butler as a relative and never called him anything except her greatest friend.

"Sometimes Mother wouldn't let us invite our student friends: it wasn't seemly for young ladies to send out invitations! Aunt would recall her youth, "and so we would go to Fedot, and give him a note overnight, he would jump on his horse, change at the first drove of horses he came to, and thus he would get all the way to town in the night and return by morning. And that day there would be visitors!"

That's the kind of flying machine he was! And not only had he done favours for the young Il'menev ladies in his time and fulfilled both the possible and the impossible for them, but he was the first servant of the young officers, as they were then—he had seen a thing or two with Alexander Pavlovich and the late Vasilii Pavlovich.

Whenever Olya took up a stand about something, and however much they all persuaded her against it, would not budge an inch, they called her Vasilii Il'menev.

The Il'menev line were all strong and tall and there wasn't one of them who complained of his chest, but Vasilii Pavlovich, even though he was an Il'menev, went and died of consumption. Their late Granny Anna Mikhailovna often used to tell all kinds of tales about her terrible hapless Vasilii and incidentally of his exemplary servant Fedot: and what was there they wouldn't do, they'd set out for town in fine style and return home on foot—having lost the carriage and horses at cards!

Nothing was ever done in Vatagino without Fedot and no event ever seemed to take place without his participation: Fedot took the liveliest part in the life of the masters he had accepted for ever. He only had one eye but his solitary green eye was sharp and he had no need of another, and thank Heaven he heard everything clearly, even to a midge bite and did not

complain of deafness. And no one had ever seen him sleep, a thing
for which thieves feared him like fire and fled from him for three
versts at the very least.

That's the kind of man Fedot the Bent was, and after the
death of Fedot the Straight, he was the only Fedot.

* * .* * *

Towards evening in the cool of the sunset Granny's heavy
Turntub with room for ten, and not second even to the Il'menevs'
Trundleteer, drove into Vatagino. And of course Fedot met
Olya by the windmill as usual.

"Well, Fedot, how are things at home?" Olya asked when
Fedot had settled down beside Granny's Konon.

"Everything's all right, Miss, thank the Good Lord, visitors
have come from town."

"For me?" Olya said happily.

"Two young ladies: Rogacheva and Protasova. And Kostya
has arrived at the Borovs' from the cadet corps, Konstantin
Anatol'evich. A letter has come from your Aunt Lyudmila
Pavlovna: they promise to come to Vatagino for Assumption. A
student tutor comes for your brother," Fedot was silent a moment and added hopelessly, " Everyone has his tastes."

Fedot smelt of the house and amid questions about things
at home the heavy Turntub rolled past Father Evdokim's, past
the Church of the Intercession of the Holy Virgin, the Perovs'
garden, Vera Streshnev's, Lena Borov's, as imperceptibly as a
light *droshki*, and the two white towers of the Il'menevs' white
house appeared.

Fedot jumped from the driving seat and lightly pushed open
the gates on to such a green, green yard in welcome to his
favourite young lady Ol'ga Alexandrovna whom all the dogs,
both the black ones and the white ones in the yard and the gentle
red hunter Cadeau, were no less delighted to see.

Hearing the tinkling bells Katya Rogachev and Leda Protasov jumped out from behind the green peas and Alexander
Pavlovich himself came out into the porch.

"Daddy, Daddy! Katya! Leda!" Olya cried, out of breath with delight at the white house and its towers and yard which was so wide and green.

The horses had not yet halted when Olya leapt down. And she fell. She got up as if nothing had happened and ran along the grass, along her native earth.

III

Olya had two constant friends in Vatagino, Vera Streshnev and Lena Borov.

Olya made friends with Vera Streshnev, when she was moved up into the VIIth form. Olya went to see Vera first and invited her home, and before this neither Olya nor Vera had been in each other's houses in spite of being neighbours. Vera was an ordinary Vatagino young lady and did not go to a High School or an Institute, but she possessed something which no schoolgirl necessarily acquires, something which is called noble-heartedness, conscientiousness and attentiveness—and it was this which attracted Olya to her.

Lena Borov, Olya had known since childhood—the Borovs were neighbours and constant visitors at the Il'menevs, just like relatives. Lena was the same age as Vera and about two years Olya's senior. She was always restless and even when she had been brought to see the Il'menevs when she was quite small there had always been a lot of trouble and fuss with her and you couldn't ever please her with anything. She didn't like this and she didn't like that and the milk was wrong and the bread.

"You'll be like Lena Borov!" Nurse Fatevna used to tell Olya when Olya began gryning, as Nurse Fatevna called it.

Lena went to a High School and when she came home for the holidays she would initiate Olya into all her pranks at school: she told her how she used to sneeze right in the teacher's ear, how she could hiccup skilfully and non-stop for a whole lesson, how she had cut off another girl's eyelashes when she was asleep and all kinds of stories like this in a very absorbing and amazing

strain for such a trusting person as Olya. Lena did not finish
school. When she was in one of the top classes she came home
for Christmas one year and something seemed to happen to her:
she had always been restless and now she became more restless
still, they said it was as if she was *possessed*, but why, no one
could make out. She never left the house except to see Olya.
And from Thursday evening to Friday evening she went nowhere: this was the most nerve-wracking day in the week for
her—she was afraid she would die. And her fears only left her
when Olya came.

Alexander Pavlovich with whom she always spoke more
freely than with other people, loved her for her restlessness and
her devils.

"She's not like other people!" he said of her.

And this was true: Lena could always say anything straight
out to anybody, whoever he was, and not just to his face but in
the presence of others—here she was not afraid and it was this
which attracted Olya to her.

* * * * *

The evening started off well.

The white table shining with the ancient Il'menev silver was
more white and silvery than ever. Perhaps it seemed so to Olya
after Mezheninka which was flowery and overgrown, or she had
been sorely homesick for this house, or the house itself was glad
of her and so had decked itself in silver as for holiday.

Besides themselves—Misha, Irena and Lena and Olya's two
school-friends, Katya Rogachev and Leda Protasov—there were
guests: of course Vera Streshnev was there and so too was Lena
Borov, and Lena's brother the cadet Kostya, the Lupechev twins
Peter and Paul and a completely new person—Misha's tutor, the
the student Karaulov.

Misha told funny stories at which he laughed himself, though
not so much as his audience did. The student Karaulov sang
couplets and though he had a weak voice he sang with great
feeling, and that was funny too, with all kinds of comic choruses.

Karaulov danced most with Olya.

Then they danced.

Alexander Pavlovich stayed with the guests all evening. He sat in the armchair by the fireplace under the clock and when they started dancing he went to dance the mazurka with Olya.

How glad he was to see her, his small kitten—that's what he called her—and how fondly he looked at her and smiled on her! And he danced as no one dances now.

"Daddy, Daddy darling, how easy it is to dance with you and how goo-ood!" Olya smiled her clear smile.

She was as full of health as the black and fruitful earth of her home was full of strong power. And her heavy plaits floated on the air like corn.

They teased the twins Peter and Paul a lot: they both had a great passion for dancing but in spite of lessons—and Alexander Pavlovich taught them himself—they could only dance one way and couldn't manage the turn. They leapt bear-like round the ballroom constantly wiping themselves with their check handkerchieves and so hard and so zealously that you'd think their skins were really warm fur.

Karaulov—Olya remembered afterwards—raced about for all he was worth and more deftly than the others, beating time with his heel and circling so fast that all pallor vanished.

Karaulov danced most with Olya.

When they had danced their fill they started parlour games.

They played "censors." The game consisted in two people chosen by lot leaving the circle: one sat as "censor" and the other collected opinions about him and then passed them on aloud to him and the person whose opinion seemed the most striking to the "censor" had to leave the circle and become the "censor" in his turn. Olya was censor and Lena was collecting opinions. When she had been round the whole circle Lena began telling Olya aloud all the opinions about her, funny ones, tender ones and ones with no connection, and none of them touched Olya except one which was really quite unlike, a verse—"Ol'ga the beautiful stumbles through the streets" and something more in the same strain.

"Whose opinion is this?" asked Olya.

No one moved in the circle as if there was no such opinion and no one to step forward.

"Who made this up?"

Olya looked round the circle and at her father who seemed to be sitting over there by the fire frowning.

"Who, then, who?"

And then, looking somehow so timid and pale (Olya remembered afterwards) Karaulov stepped forward. He should have walked up to Olya but he had not taken a step when Alexander Pavlovich got up from the armchair under the clock.

And for some reason everything grew very still—you could hear the grasshoppers chirruping in the garden outside.

Karaulov turned and stooping walked quickly from the room.

And from that evening he did not come to the Il'menevs' house any more.

IV

Ksaverii Matveevich's son, the student Lampad, came from Lubenetzi to invite Olya and her friends for a picnic in the Lubenetzi forest. Lubenetzi was quite near, halfway between Vatagino and Mezheninka.

Lampad pressed Natalya Ivanovna and the girls assured her that Ksaverii Matveevich and Alexandra Kensorinovna would certainly be there too. So they let Olya and her friends go, with injunctions not to return too late and to be careful with the horses.

They had a good time on the way but it was better still in the woods.

To be sure neither Ksaverii Matveevich nor Alexandra Kensorinovna were present, but Doctor Andrei Fedorovich—the "Quail," Lampad himself and his sister Asklipiodota were there. They recited verses, Andrei Fedorovich told wonderful stories about his student days which Olya fully believed. Lampad did extraordinary tricks.

And the evening went by unnoticed, they ate their *kasha** and the fire went out.

Well, they said their goodbyes and set off—Olya, Katya and Leda—and eventually they arrived home. And late, such a late hour had never even entered anyone's head—the sun had already risen well above the Il'menevs' white towers and Olya's stork had flown off for food.

And they slept all the sounder!

But when the morning came worry took the place of sleep.

They decided that Leda should go into breakfast first—Leda Protasov was quieter than Katya and people had more confidence in her—she would make some excuse: explain things.

Of course Natalya Ivanovna was very displeased: to come home so late!

"The horses were late," Leda said, flushing red. "Ksaverii Matveevich and Alexandra Kensorinovna are very sorry."

Here Olya entered the dining-room, followed by Katya.

And Natalya Ivanovna calmed down a good deal during the ensuing conversation.

Whilst the talk was all about the Lubenetzi picnic, what a good time they had in the woods, how Ksaverii Matveevich himself went with them and Alexandra Kensorinovna, how they made a camp-fire and how Ksaverii Matveevich sang by the fire and told them funny things.

"From Holy Writ!" Katya added wickedly and burst out laughing.

And they all started laughing but not at the same thing which had started Katya off: not at Ksaverii Matveevich singing by the fire—if you could only have seen Ksaverii Matveevich even when he wasn't singing!—nor at Holy Writ taking the place of Lampad's tricks and the Quail's anecdotes, not this set them

---

* *Kasha*—a kind of porridge made with rye, in which the grains are separate and less moist than with oatmeal. *Translator's Note.*

laughing, but it was a lovely day and it was lovely that everything had ended so happily and Natalya Ivanovna had quite given over scolding and was smiling at Olya.

"Mummy, you must understand how happy we were!" Olya answered with her clear smile.

After the heat of the day from which you could but hide in the rooms behind shutters, just as soon as the evening breeze began to blow, Olya ran out into the garden with Leda and Katya after her. They had a swing and then went for a walk. They went to the windmill, once a forbidden place, and further into the fields. They picked great big bunches of flowers—if Olya set herself to do something the result was always superabundant.

They went with their flowers, themselves like the wild flowers of the field.

Warm summer stars came out into the heavenly fields.

"My blessing is upon you!" was wafted in the air.

When they got to the church they started hurrying: mustn't be late for supper!

They ran back home and the first thing they saw in the yard was the "Apostles"—that's what Ksaverii Matveevich called the oxen with which he drove out on visits to his neighbours. That meant it was Ksaverii Matveevich! Their hearts sank into their boots: what about the picnic now, with the old man singing and telling funny things . . . from Holy Writ?

Dropping their flowers, they went in.

In the dining-room Ksaverii Matveevich was sitting by the samovar and blithely finishing his usual unchangeable story about how in his youth, driving out once on the first day of Easter to pay calls, his carriage got stuck in front of a girls' school, and about how he was extricated.

And as usual Alexandra Kensorinovna heard it out with unchanging attention as if it was a new tale, this terrible accident, and she nodded sympathetically from time to time.

"And we just left the thing there!" the narrator, waving his hand, usually ended his story.

"Well, and how was the picnic, Ksaverii Matveevich?" Natalya Ivanovna asked.

"How can we keep up with the young ones!   We old people are best without picnics and we enjoy sitting at home most of all."

Next day Leda Protasov went home to the Protasov estate.

And soon after this Lubenetzi picnic Natalya Ivanovna made preparations to go to Mezheninka.

Olya refused to go, point-blank.   And she wouldn't give in to any persuasions—an absolute Vasilii Il'menev!   She couldn't do otherwise: if she went, Katya too would have to leave Vatagino and Katya had fallen in love with the cadet Kostya and was ready to extend her visit to the Il'menevs for the whole summer.

Olya didn't know for what reasons and why, Katya was considered an unsuitable friend among the girls of her circle. Olya was told she was not her equal and at one time she was not even allowed in her house.   And it was this prohibition which bound Olya to Katya the scatterbrain as Katya called herself.

To stay at home on Katya's account and not go with the whole family to her favourite Granny in Mezheninka, cost Olya a great deal.

And when the Il 'menevs' Trundleteer with Natalya Ivanovna, Irena, Lena and Misha was lost to sight behind the black poplar and the house felt so empty and deserted, Olya and Katya went to the hayloft, sat down side by side and cried till evening.

V

On Mr. Borov's saintsday (he was Lena's father) the Borovs had their one great celebration of the year—the whole of Vatagino made merry.

Alexander Pavlovich who usually avoided parties of every kind, went to the Borovs' solely to please Olya.

"Do you know who wants to see you?" Lena whispered.

"Who?"

"Karaulov."

"Karaulov?" Olya had not given the student a thought the whole week.

He wants to apologise. He would have come here only he's afraid to. He's at the Perovs'."

Lena led Olya away from the guests across the balcony. And they went through the garden gate into the Perovs' garden.

Karaulov was ready waiting and very nervous.

"It was just quite childish how it happened . . . my verses that night."

"I don't mind at all," Olya began to feel uncomfortable herself—after all she didn't blame him for anything. "It's just father: he was very offended with you that time on my account."

Karaulov was happy: Olya didn't blame him and that was everything. Lena took him aside saying something and he listened respectfully.

Then they left the garden.

"You know, Olya, Karaulov is staying with the Streshnevs. Vera told me he wept the whole week."

Next day Karaulov went round to the Il'menevs' and sat a long time with Alexander Pavlovich. And when Natalya Ivanovna returned from Mezheninka, Misha had to settle down to his books again and Karaulov came to the house once more.

There was a custom in the Il'menev family for the girls to take it in turns to pour out tea: one day Irena would do it, the next Olya and then Lena.

Olya never poured out. Karaulov did it for her and he fulfilled a hostess's duties with exceptional tact, handling the teacups with as much gentleness as he handled his white mice.

Little was known of Karaulov's life and it somehow never entered anyone's head to enquire. They merely knew that he had no mother, only a stepmother.

"Is your stepmother young?" Natalya Ivanovna once asked him.

"She was young once," Karaulov answered.

He usually answered in this vein, but a different voice and

different words came to him when he was talking to Olya. His grey eyes would grow dark. And it always seemed to Olya when he spoke to her that he was in pain.

It bored Olya to pour out tea, so Karaulov did it for her. Olya liked getting letters and the letters usually piled up in the post office for a long time, and Karaulov would go on foot to town when it was hardly light, so that as soon as Olya got up, he would be back and Olya would have her letters in good time.

Karaulov left the Streshnev's where he had rented a room, and settled down at the Il'menev's, in a hut in the garden. He studied with Misha in the mornings, in the afternoon he went off into the fields with a book, in the evenings he stayed with the family and after evening tea he went off to his hut.

They often had parties in the evenings. The Lupechev twins Peter and Paul would come and of course Vera Streshnev and Lena Borov too, and her brother the cadet Kostya. They would dance, tell funny stories, sing and play games.

The time went by merrily.

And Karaulov was the heart and soul of all their projects and amusements.

And he tried to please Olya best of all.

What amusing boats he made her from the bark of trees!

When they were not with the others but alone, Karaulov told Olya about himself, about his interests, the university, his lectures, professors and fellow-students. He was going through the second course already and, wishing to get a grasp of the whole field of knowledge, he had changed his special subject several times in his first year: he had started with Botany and had studied the classification of plants diligently with Gorozhankin, then he left classification and buried himself in crustaceans and arachnida with Zograff, got through an enormous tome, went to Stoletov and got tied up in Physics formulae and now he was trying to make up his mind whether to stop with birds at Menzbir's or to go over to the faculty of Law and study Jurisprudence with Novgorodtsev.

"I don't believe in God," he told Olya once.

And this surprised her greatly: it had never even entered her head that you could say such things and so lightly.

"I don't believe in God," Karaulov would repeat every time Olya began to talk on her favourite curious theme.

And when Olya would say her prayers and pray for her father and mother, for her brother, her sisters and her favourite granny, and these words came to her, she would pray for him too, that the student Karaulov should believe in God.

VI

They saw Katya Rogachev off on St. Elijah's Day. She parted from the cadet Kostya without a tremor, or the shadow of a tear in her mischievous eye: she had fallen in love that spring during the exams with a boy in the VIIIth form, Ponomar'kov, whom she was soon to see again now and the thought of this meeting excited her feelings.

Karaulov, after a clever biological dissertation during which he showed Olya his white mice, asked her to give him a photograph of herself. Olya promised on condition he would give her one of himself too. He was ready to do anything for her if it came to that and as soon as he arrived in Moscow he would have one taken and send it to her. He repeated this about ten times. And when Olya gave him her photograph there was no end to his happiness—he sang all evening, and all night in his hut as well.

"The student-teacher has gone off his head completely," Fedot said in the servants' hall. "If you go and see him in his hut, he isn't asleep, he walks the garden like a bird, and such craziness: 'Fedot Prokhorovich,' he says, 'would you like me to fix you up with a duck's eye?' Crazy!"

And it was true, when he got Olya's photograph, Karaulov went like a bird for three days and probably didn't sleep at night.

One evening at tea, before he had touched his own glass even, he suddenly started hurrying and asked Olya to get him a book—Olya always had charge of the key to the library. And when Olya left the dining-room with him, he gave her a letter and without waiting for the book, went off.

He hadn't wanted any book!

The letter was a very long one: in fine characters, carefully written, all about his feelings—his love for Olya, with expectations and promises and avowals, well, an explanatory love-letter, how he would marry Olya and they would live together. And at the end he begged Olya not to forget him while he was finishing his studies at the university.

"And when I finish, please God, our fate will be resolved."

Which of us doesn't find pleasure in a love-letter?

Olya was very pleased.

She first discovered that boys fell in love with her when she was in the Vth form. And at balls when the third quadrille came—the third quadrille is a special one, signifying love—Olya simply didn't know whom to choose: she had so many invitations. Besides that, Misha used to tell her who had a pash for her, as the schoolboys and schoolgirls called it—Misha was *persona grata* in the punishment room and the punishment room was certainly the place for heart-to-heart talks! And there were boys whom she would meet wherever she went—on the way to school and on the way back, at church—wherever it was they would meet and, of course, not by chance.

In the VIIth form she had her first avowal. The seventh-former Dagestansky, nicknamed "Bullock," gave Olya his photograph with the inscription "from your l . . . . Leonid Dagestansky." And when Olya took the card he had kissed her hand.

By the time Olya reached the VIIIth form cards just like this took up a whole corner of the jewel box where she kept her treasures.

Which of us does not find pleasure in an avowal of love! Olya was very pleased.

But she had never written anything on her own card to anyone.

Next day at evening tea, again with a book as a pretext,

Karaulov got Olya out of the room with him, and gave her another letter, going off himself.

The letter consisted of a few lines but in the same fine script, carefully written: he asked Olya to come and talk to him in the hayloft at four o'clock the next morning.

Olya knew from Katya that the hayloft was a rendezvous in Vatagino, and that Katya and Cadet Kostya had been there, but she didn't dream of going: at such an unearthly hour—Olya liked to spoil herself a bit, to lie in of a morning, and here was a bidding to appear at 4 a.m.!

She got several other letters like this with the one request: for a talk in the hayloft.

"I heard such a thing about Karaulov!" Lena said.

"What?"

"You can't imagine: he's very ill. Kostya told me about the awful attacks he gets, specially when he's very worried about something."

Olya and Lena were walking back from church through the garden. The first autumnal morning was changing into a red sabbath day. Lena was telling Olya, on Kostya's authority, about the attacks Karaulov had, how he got contorted and foamed at the mouth and how frightening it was.

Olya listened very attentively. She would never have thought it.

"Why does he get these attacks?"

But Lena had not time to reply when they heard a cry behind them and they fell apart. Karaulov was flailing about on the gravel path and it was terrifying.

Olya thought he was dying and rushed off to the house to find someone.

But Karaulov recovered very soon, only he was very melancholy and when he talked to Olya his grey eyes got darker than ever, and she felt more strongly than before that something was hurting him. He couldn't but notice the change—Olya was so attentive!—and he recovered his spirits.

The summer was drawing to a close. It was time to finish

lessons with Misha, for Karaulov to go back to the university in Moscow and for Olya to return to school.

At one of the farewell parties they were playing "Enigmas" and Olya got a note—in fine script carefully written. Karaulov asked her what did Olya like best about him?

Olya wanted to answer truthfully that she felt how much his being ill touched her—she always treated sick people differently—but she changed her mind and didn't say that, instead she wrote:

"Eyebrows, eyes and eyelashes."

And indeed he did have beautiful eyes, brows and lashes.

On the eve of his departure, Karaulov said goodbye after evening tea and went off to his hut. Olya and Lena followed him out on to the porch.

It was an autumn night, full of stars.

Stars, starlets, starry ways in every direction.

Fedot, clanking his keys, passed along the yard with a lantern on his way to the storehouses. A black dog ran after Fedot in the light. A cold breeze came from the garden.

And a star shot through the night.

"I love you so!" Karaulov said very softly and he kissed Olya's hand.

VII

Aunt Lyudmila Pavlovna arrived in Vatagino for Assumption as she had promised. She installed herself in one of the towers of the old Il'menev house where she had spent the days of her unforgettable youth. And her vivid memory of the past brought the old Il'menev days back to life: after all, in her eyes, Alexander Pavlovich was still her younger brother Sasha, and there had been another brother Vasya, and Kolya her favourite.

"My inestimable friend and brother, Nikolai Pavlovich," she had invariably begun those long letters of hers to him in St. Petersburg, and she would conclude after all wishes for his health, happiness and best possible fortune, "I would like to send you my heart, but cannot, and would be glad if someone would transmit my thoughts to you, for I cannot now."

Opening the piano Lyudmila Pavlovna would recall the grief of her girlhood years.

"And if I feel heavy at heart," she said, "I sit down to play and when the tears come, I feel relief."

Olya was very fond of questioning her aunt about how things had been in their family formerly, about what her father had been like when he was small, and about Grandfather and Grandmother. And now her aunt had come she put off her departure for another day.

And the day passed quietly in conversation and recollection.

Next day Olya started getting ready for the journey in the morning and towards evening everything was ready.

Vera Streshnev and Lena Borov came. They all went into the ballroom together in the customary way, sat still a moment silent and then all rose together. Olya followed Natalya Ivanovna and Alexander Pavlovich to the miracle-working Il'menev ikon of the Mother of God. They said a prayer. And then bade each other farewell.

Nurse Fatevna who was recently returned from a pilgrimage to a far-off shrine, sprinkled Olya with holy water of Gennesareth.

They said goodbye once more and Olya kissed everyone over again.

Natalya Ivanovna cried a little.

"Mummy, my darling Mummy!" and Olya kissed her a long time.

But you couldn't take her tears away.

"Be sure and call at Granny's!" she said through her tears and followed Olya out.

They all came.

And Olya, flushed and smiling her clear smile, kissed them all again and again, and said goodbye in the servants' hall and on the porch once more and for the last time as she got in.

Alexander Pavlovich went with Olya as far as the windmill. He made the sign of the cross over his small kitten, as he called

Olya, Fedot settled down next to Gregory and they were off.

And Fedot went with Olya as far as Lubenetzi, as far as Ksaverii Matveevich's.

He told Olya how he used to go—it was a long time now—with Alexander Pavlovich and the late Vasilii Pavlovich when they went to school, and what they were like and how free and easy things were then.

"Ekh, what a man!" the one-eyed butler would add, intoning the words rather than saying them.

He passed from their schooldays to later times when the Il'menevs were young officers. His military tales were so absorbing that even Gregory the coachman, with his peacock feather and in his long sleeveless drugget coat over a poppy-red shirt, an old man himself, would whistle bravely not so much to the horses as out of sheer enjoyment.

"Ekh, what a man!"

Olya arrived betimes in Mezheninka, they weren't thinking of bed yet and were setting the table leisurely for supper. And as usual, Olya's arrival created an upheaval.

What happiness unending! Granny, Aunt and Anna Pavovna were nearly rushed off their feet in their delight. Of course there was no question of Olya leaving next day or the day after either.

So Olya spent several days with her favourite Granny.

*   *   *   *   *

It was quiet in Mezheninka and full of loving-kindness.

Life flowed on unhurried as it had done for many years, one day quietly after another.

Autumn called for remarks about winter. Aunt Evgenia Alexeyevna was fussing about with putty at the window in the corner to the right of the image-case, where she liked to lay out her patience in the evenings, putting in the winter frames.

They had laid in a not inconsiderable store against winter. Granny led Olya to the storeroom ... What jam! And how many jars, big and small, there were, bearing labels in Granny's hand:

> Olya's raspberry.
> Olyushka's favourite raspberry.
> Olya's strawberry.
> Olyushka's favourite strawberry.
> Olya's peach.
> Olyushka's white cherry.
> Olya's barberry, stoneless.

"A grub got all the eating apples," Granny bewailed, "and there are no apples of our kind or the Chinese this year. But Aunt still has a whole heap of last year's."

Aunt Evgenia Alexeyevna wouldn't give anyone any of her jam, so there was no point in asking, and now to Granny's disappointment, Olya wouldn't get any of her favourite jam—Olya's apple.

From the storeroom Granny took Olya to the little storeroom where all the salted things were and there was a lovely smell. Here she made Olya a present of a bottle of *eau-de-cologne* which she had distilled herself and revealed the whole secret of the recipe for Olya's sole benefit.

Olya had a good memory and she had no need to write it down, she would remember without that, and would make Granny not a bottle but a whole pail of *eau-de-cologne*.

Unhurriedly, the way everything was done in Mezheninka, Granny went through the ingredients, enumerating the quantities and the things you had to put in, spirit of wine, purified till it lost the smell of liquor completely and the different oils: bergamot pear, lemon, rosemary, gillyflower and orange blossom.

"You must put all these things in the spirit in a large flagon, shake it well, and your *eau-de-cologne* will be ready. It will be cloudy at first but will settle in a few days and when it is quite clear, you must decant it carefully and strain the dregs through paper. When the *eau-de-cologne* is ready you pour it into bottles and tie the tops down. The longer it's left to stand the more mature it will get."

Over evening tea they recalled the old days when Granny was young and Aunt was young and Anna Pavlovna. First Granny, then Aunt and then Anna Pavlovna.

Anna Pavlovna did not miss the opportunity of telling how General Ol'hovsky proposed to her and she refused him. Olya couldn't restrain herself and began arguing. As always, this annoyed Granny.

And then afterwards they made it all up.

> "Ach, what a pity,
> That clothes so pretty
> Are no more worn today;
> Soon the shawl
> And veil and all
> We'll in the cupboard lay . . ."

Anna Pavlovna, unfortunate in all respects, began to hum.

Olya asked Granny about things in the old days, about Mummy when she was small, and Kostroma.

Granny did not reply immediately.

"Wait a moment!" Granny always began and she gazed with such kind clear eyes. "That happened at the Ryazanovskys, no, not at the Ryazanovskys, they lived in the Tsarevskaya and our house was in the Rusinaya . . ." And in this way she would slowly get to the most important theme, about the old days, the days of her youth when great events took place in the world.

"It was better in the old days," Granny, Aunt and Anna Pavlovna all agreed.

And was it really true that Granny, Aunt and Anna Pavlovna had once been young!

> "Ach, what a pity
> That clothes so pretty
> Are no more worn today;
> Soon the shawl
> And veil and all
> We'll in the cupboard lay . . ."

* * * * *

It was quiet in Mezheninka and full of loving-kindness.

Olya would have liked to stay longer—look what a golden garden, what asters, what nights there were!—but it was impossible: it was time, time for Olya to go to school.

"When I used to have to go home," Granny recalled as she saw Olya off, "you'd start crying at the top of your voice and nothing would quiet you, I remember, and, I remember, I gave you silver pieces to amuse you, I'd go on giving them to you till you had I don't know how many, and you'd still go on crying and wouldn't let me go. I could only get away by deceiving you somehow. And now it's I who shed tears."

Granny's heavy Turntub, to the great interest of the Mezheninka hens and turkeys, stood a long while by the porch, so that the hens and turkeys got quite used to it and went on without paying any attention as before, and Granny's Konon even had a nap, while they were decking Olya out for the journey and saying goodbye again and again and again as before at home.

"Till Christmas, Granny!"

Olya kept turning round and smiling her clear smile, until the heavy Turntub took the bend by the church and was lost to view.

And the three of them stood in the wide porch; one, taller and stouter than the others—Granny, the other, all bone, flashing her great dark eyes once so beautiful and now so menacing—Aunt, and the third, the smallest and most unfortunate—Anna Pavlovna.

"And when you drove away, Olyushka, my friend, "Granny wrote to Olya at school, "I felt quite crazed, cried and tormented my heart, worrying about you. Your Granny till the grave, Tatiana Alexeyevna."

VIII

Olya often got letters from Karaulov in Moscow, and they were all long ones like the first, written in small characters with great care.

He described all his hopes and disappointments—his whole life: he had changed from the History of Jurisprudence to Mercantile Law and from Mercantile Law to Chemistry, from Yanzhul to Sabaneev, and was going to do Inorganic and Organic Chemistry before going to Klyuchevsky's lectures. And all his letters were permeated with his unchanging love and hopes of the happy future which Olya was to decide. She got his photograph too——

"In memory of a hot summer."

Olya wrote to him about twice and very briefly.

She didn't like writing letters at the best of times, but besides this, each of Karaulov's letters (and the more loving they were the stronger the feeling they roused in her) oppressed her with the heavy weight of this right he had assumed to send her letters like this, to hope and expect something of her, and this weight on her heart was turning into irritation and even into hatred.

She counted her friends happy because, as she thought, no one wrote to them like that nor had the right to, and they were alone and free. Her one desire—she would do anything, anything at all to achieve this—was to get rid of him and of his right over her.

And the more this weight on her mind gave place to irritation and hatred, the more she felt an aversion from him gaining a grip on her.

How happy she had been before all these letters! And how happy she would be when she was rid of them!

And so she made up her mind, whatever happened, to see Karaulov and to get back her letters and her photograph, and to end it all that way.

Then it would all end.

A chance offered itself, not very soon it was true, but it did come.

The students usually came down for the Christmas vacation a long time before Christmas. And Karaulov arrived at the very beginning of December.

Olya lived with the Zubarevs when she was in the VIIIth form. Alexandra Timofeevna Zubarev, a doctor's wife, was a friend of Natalya Ivanovna's. Olya was well looked after in her house and had no restrictions: she was treated like a grown-up—an VIIIth form girl!

Learning that Karaulov had arrived, Olya wrote to ask him to come and see her on Sunday. But unknown to her, tickets had been taken for the opera on Sunday.

After dinner Alexandra Timofeevna and Olya went for a walk and were out for quite a long while—when they got back Karaulov was already there.

Karaulov was waiting for Olya.

Olya came in from the cold as cold as an icicle and she had on a red jumper. He was delighted to see her and started asking her what she was thinking about and how she was passing the time.

Alexandra Timofeevna told Olya to hurry: Olya had to change.

And when she was ready—she had not time to say a word to him—the three of them left together.

Snatching a moment Olya told him what she had had in mind all this time and her reason for asking him to call: he must give back her letters and her photograph.

"Are you quite certain you want them?" Karaulov stopped.

"Quick! Give them to me quickly," Olya hurried him.

He unbuttoned his coat, pushed his hand inside, pulled out an envelope and handed it to Olya.

Alexandra Timofeevna had taken a cab and was calling Olya: she was very worried in case they would be late. Olya hurried across to her. When she looked back he was already gone.

But Olya did not give the matter another thought. Olya loved music and was delighted with the opera, she was ready to go every day if necessary.

On Monday the Zubarevs got tickets for the opera again and Olya and Alexandra Timofeevna went again.

After the opera they were sitting over tea and the doctor, Alexandra Timofeevna's husband, was telling them all the town gossip, when he remarked among other things:

"Such a catastrophe! This morning they brought a student who hanged himself round to the hospital . . . Karaulov. He tried to buy a revolver but they wouldn't sell him one, so he hanged himself in his lodgings."

"Karaulov? The name sounds familiar!" Alexandra Timofeevna said.

But Olya did not say a word. Olya didn't want them to see, and something cold crept over her.

She walked shivering up and down her room all night.

She went over it all—the first happy evening party, "Censors," the whole summer. "Are you quite certain you want them?"—kept repeating and repeating in her mind, with his strong accent on "certain." But she had not had a chance to ask him anything, she didn't know anything and perhaps she was not the cause? She had not had a chance to ask him anything!

The thought that perhaps she was not the cause of it but something else, quietened her a little and towards morning she fell asleep.

And she had a dream—she dreamt she saw a grave with a great cross and she knew that this was Karaulov's grave. She sat down on the grave and she heard a voice coming from the grave:

"Oh, how heavy the weight is!"

1909 - 1921.